THE LIAR

John P. Murphy

Thank you for reading!

https://www.johnpmurphy.net

ISBN-13:978-1724667977
ISBN-10:1724667971

IT WAS THE END OF OCTOBER IN VERSAILLES, New Hampshire, and the world smelled of wood smoke. The leaf peepers had come and gone for the season, and the last of the die-hard kayakers were shivering on Scorn Pond and telling themselves all that beauty was worth a little discomfort. Business was slow so I had an apple pie in the oven—my latest attempt at getting it right—and I was raking leaves. The pie was probably tempting fate, seeing as I tend to get visitors out of the blue and I'm kind of the distractible type. Folks up here think I'm the local handyman, and that's true enough as it goes, but it would be more accurate to say that I'm the town liar.

I lived alone in the house I grew up in and figured that because it's what I always pictured, it was what I always wanted. My old house is up on the hill overlooking the southern part of town. Not much to look *at*, though, Versailles, not like its namesake. Comes from pronouncing it to rhyme with "sails," I expect. A little too sparse to be picturesque and a little too settled to be bucolic. It's an old town and it shows, but it's about right for me.

I gave the rake a tug and there was a sharp crack. I plucked off my canvas gloves and knelt down—not a thing I do lightly on a cool fall day, but not anything I worry overmuch about yet, either—and inspected the broken bamboo spoke. It'd stuck in the ground, and the rake was old, and I hadn't been any too gentle. The tine broke off in one piece, though: ought to be an easy lie.

I brushed away the dirt and fitted it back together as tight as I could. "Looks solid to me," I muttered. "Ayuh, must have been mistaken. That ain't broke at all." I waggled it carefully to illustrate my point. "Couldn't do that if it were broke," I continued, picturing it as one long, strong piece. "No, and I wouldn't do it if it were cracked. Wouldn't make sense, would it? Must be fine, seems to me."

I hauled myself back up onto my feet and inspected the result. Looked solid, but then I *had* to think that. I shook the rake head and it rattled but nothing fell off. Good enough for now. Later on I'd tell it something a little more convincing, or hell, just find the superglue. Solid enough to finish the yard, anyway.

I heard Pastor Julie's truck before I saw it come around the bend. She was still driving an ancient Chevy that didn't have an "unleaded fuel only" warning. It was a kind of barn red that I don't believe was strictly automotive paint. Every time I look at it, I give the fender a good whack and marvel out loud how sturdy it is after all these years. Pastor Julie knows better than to contradict me on that score, least not out loud, even though she doesn't know why. A fella like me gets a reputation for knowing these things, and she picked up on it pretty fast despite being new in town.

She didn't see me standing off to the side; I could tell because she never swears when she thinks people can hear her. I couldn't see what she was doing after she stopped and turned off the engine, so I wasn't sure what prompted the chorus of scatology until she put her phone to her ear. Daughter Ashley, by my guess, up to something teenagery. I raked away from the truck so as to give her some privacy.

As it happened, it was only a minute before she yelled, "Greg!" I turned and took off my floppy-brimmed hat and waved it at her. She jammed her phone into her jeans pocket and waved back, favoring me with a broad smile. "Missed you in church."

She always says that, because she figures she has to, and I always say, "Nice to be missed."

"Yard's looking good. You going to mow again, or you think we're done for the season?"

I studied her for a moment under the guise of thinking over her question. She'd gotten some sun and had a few more freckles. They looked good on her. She was peering out at the grass but I could tell she was paying attention to me. She wanted a favor, which was fine, because I liked doing favors for Pastor Julie, but usually she came right out with it.

"Yuh, once more, I think. Take down the mower blade a notch and cut it close."

She nodded at the rake. "Why don't you just mow it all?"

I looked at her askance. "I don't mow leaves. Makes a mess. Not good for the mower." She knew it, of course. Everybody knows it. Questions like that reminded everyone she wasn't from around here, and while Boston isn't as bad as, say, New York, it was still Away.

"I like my mulching mower. Goes right through them like butter." She made a driving motion with both hands. "No point in raking, anyway. Ashley's been too old to jump in the pile for years."

I pulled a plastic bag out of my back pocket. "Here, make yourself useful."

"I like to think I'm inherently useful," she said with that grin of hers as she unfolded the bag and shook it open. By the time I had an armful of leaves up, she was holding it open like a basket to take them.

"Tried your cell," she said, "I didn't get through."

I nodded. The Infernal Device was on my kitchen table, so I could prove to anyone who came by that I had one and it worked and I was in point of fact living in the twenty-first century. Its battery was probably dead, though, seeing as I never plugged it in. The real telephone had rung at some point but I'd been too far from the house to get to it. Besides, I'm pretty sure Pastor Julie liked the opportunity to come up and chat in person. Old South Logging Road was a nice drive in most weather, especially so with some color on the trees.

"Sorry about that," I said. "Did you need something?"

"As a matter of fact, I do. Kind of a big

something, but it pays."

"Yuh?"

"I suppose you heard about Joe MacDevitt."

I deposited another armload of leaves, peered into the half-full bag, and gave it a push to see how much more would fit. Joe was the town cemetery caretaker. Tough old bird, in his seventies or eighties; makes a cup of coffee strong enough to stand a spoon up in. I fix his fence pretty much every year around Halloween and listen to him go on about "kids these days." I am not an unsympathetic audience, despite being thirty years his junior and probably included among the "kids."

"No, I can't say I have. He all right?"

"Thank God, yes. He was up late digging a grave yesterday evening and his back went out."

"Oh no."

She nodded, lips pursed. "He was lying there for hours, in the grave, before Chief Dulac drove by in his cruiser and saw the gate open. Even so, that was after midnight."

"Poor Joe. But you said he's all right?"

"I don't know the details. Doctor Tremblay was talking about sending him to the regional hospital, but either he changed his mind or Joe bullied him out of it, because Joe's at home now resting. Anyway, I paid a couple of Ashley's friends from school to finish the grave, but Joe's not going to be able to continue on as sexton."

"I see."

"It's not much extra work, Greg, otherwise Joe would've had to quit years ago. And you don't *have* to dig the graves yourself: there's money for that, and there's a backhoe. Just some lawn mowing and record keeping, and scheduling. And the position does pay a little."

I bit my lip. It was not, I had to admit, a terrible idea. And I liked working a backhoe. I packed down the third armful of leaves and she helped me tie off the bag.

"You don't have to say yes or no right now, Greg, but I did talk it over with Father Michaels already." Michaels is the Catholic priest at St. Thomas More on the far side of town. "We need someone reliable, and anyway you're practically next door."

She pointed down the hill. With the trees half-bare I could see the corner of the cemetery extension's stone walls. I thought about the extra work and the walk up and down the hill— or the drive around, if I was feeling lazy or the weather wasn't cooperating. Not too bad, really.

When I didn't respond right away, she

asked, "Do you want to grab dinner so you get a chance to ask questions?"

I'd've liked to have dinner with Pastor Julie. Quite a bit, come to think of it, but I knew she was awfully busy and I felt bad for holding out so that she felt like she had to sacrifice her time just to persuade me. As a single parent, she didn't have it easy. "Oh, I don't want to be a bother. I know you have Ashley to look after."

"Brunch?"

I grinned at her. "I'm not sure you're allowed to use the word 'brunch' north of the Massachusetts state line, y'know. Nashua, tops."

"Fine," she said, and swatted at me. "I can ask someone else, I just thought I'd give you the option."

"That's not what I meant…" I said, a little too hastily.

"I'm on to you, Greg. You're not as old and cranky as you want people to think."

"Old but not cranky," I said. "And I prefer 'curmudgeonly,' if it's all the same to you."

"You're barely older than me, Gregory Kellogg. Are you saying *I'm* old?"

She challenged me with a raised eyebrow, but she'd pulled that one before and this time I had an answer.

"Not at all. The definition of 'young' is officially 'younger than me,' so you're in the clear."

She gave me a mock-wary look and a little smile. She opened her mouth to respond, and I could tell by the twinkle in her eye that it was going to be a zinger, when her phone rang. I didn't know what jangly song that was but I recognized it as the ring tone for her daughter. Even if I hadn't, I'd have recognized the reaction: she tensed up and looked simultaneously worried and harried.

"I'm sorry, I have to take this. Give me a call and let me know what you decide." Her next word was "hello" and it wasn't to me, so I held back and let her half-jog away to her truck.

I watched her go for a while, until I couldn't hear her old Chevy anymore, and by the time that happened I found myself mentally rearranging my schedule to make room. I'd have to talk to Joe, of course, and make sure it was all right with him. But I'd already settled into picturing myself doing it, which was most of the way to a "yes."

I was halfway back to the porch when the smoke alarm went off.

Well, damn it. I knew the pie was tempting fate.

I TOOK THE HALF OF the pie that hadn't boiled over or burned, on a plate that fit in a flat box that used to hold two dozen store-brand orange sodas, and drove down the hill and into town to Joe MacDevitt's place. He had a little white house not far from the town green, and his blue Oldsmobile was parked in the gravel driveway.

"Hey, Joe!" I banged on the door and listened intently. I banged again and was pretty sure I heard a, "Come in, already!" so I barged in.

Joe's living room was cozy. I'd only seen it from the front door before, picking up keys. He had a big, beat-up leather recliner and a small TV that I'd be worried about knocking off its stand if I opened the recliner all the way. The couch looked like a refugee from the 1970s, and the coffee table was covered with fishing tackle—judging by the smell, not entirely cleaned after last use. He'd probably been getting ready for ice fishing up on Lake Umbagog.

"I'm in back!"

He didn't sound like he was on death's door, at least. His bedroom was off the small hallway decorated with old photos in round frames: his kids and his late wife Millie. The door was open and I could see him lying in bed, turned to watch the TV, but I rapped on the doorframe anyway.

"Hey, Greg, come on in." He lifted the remote and the talking heads got quiet fast as he repeatedly mashed the volume button instead of pressing mute. "Thanks for coming by. How're your folks?"

I paused to consider Joe. He knew my parents, of course, but I hadn't talked with him much about them, and one can never be too careful on the subject. New Hampshire natives are split on the subject of retiring to Florida. Some consider it a treason, a surrender to the cold and snow; they speak of retirees as of the dead or the disgraced. Others think of Florida as a kind of Yankee Valhalla, a just reward for a lifetime of early rising and snow shoveling and windshield scraping.

"They're all right. Talked to my mother the other day. It's warm."

He grunted. "Whatcha got there?"

"My latest experiment." I pulled off the dish towel and displayed the half-moon that had bled cooked apples all over the plate. The crust was crushed and flaked where I'd cut away the rest. It just generally looked like a dog had been at it, really, but it smelled good.

"Kind of a mess."

I explained the boil-over incident, and he snorted. There were plates in the cupboard and forks in the top drawer and cheese in the fridge, and he said all that like an invitation so I went and dished up two slices and put a healthy chunk of sharp cheddar on each plate. I sat down in the straight-backed chair next to the bed and balanced my plate on my knee. Joe dug in right away, getting a little cheese on the fork with the first bite of pie. He chewed thoughtfully, his wrinkled face moving like an accordion.

"Don't like cinnamon," he said at last, "but it ain't bad. What makes it an experiment?"

I explained that this crust was all-butter, as opposed to part-butter and part-shortening, or ideally part-butter and part-lard, but all the lard at Doug's was hydrogenated, so you might as well use Crisco. And if I was going to learn how to bake a proper apple pie, I was going to do it right.

"Never known a fella so interested in making pie."

"Well, seeing as I'm living alone, and I'm awfully interested in eating pie but none too interested in buying it, baking it just seems sensible."

Joe ate another forkful of pie and a bigger bite of cheese. "When I was your age, I had a different answer to that problem. You talked to that new lady pastor lately?"

"Well," I said carefully. It was never clear what some of the older folks in town meant when they said "lady pastor." She'd become a minister a few years after her husband died, and Versailles was her first posting. Being new and being female were two strikes against her for some of them. "I have, now you mention it. This morning. She told me about your accident."

He eyed me a while in silence. "Huh." He ran his tongue over his teeth, still watching me. "It's like that, then. Can't say I'm surprised, I suppose."

"What's Doc Tremblay say?"

Joe snorted. "He said if I picked up a shovel again, I'd be a damned fool." He took another bite of pie, grinding the crust with the side of his fork and stabbing it hard enough I thought he'd drop the plate. "Wanted to send me out Dartmouth-Hitchcock, if you believe it," he said with his mouth full. "Stuff and nonsense." He swallowed. "A three-hour ambulance ride. Who'd pay for that, I'd like to know?"

"Well, you're home now."

"And for a long while, from the sounds of it. They want you to take over." He said it outright, not as a question.

"I don't know if they mean it to be anything permanent. Probably just want someone to keep an eye on the place until you're back on your feet. I did want to ask you about it first, though."

He stared. "You didn't say yes?"

"Well, not yet."

"Jeeze Louise, Greg." He shook his head, sighed to himself, and looked me in the eye. "Say yes."

"All right, all right. Sure, I'll do it."

"Don't tell me, idiot, tell her."

I ate some more of my pie and let that be. He finished his, too, and I carried the plates back to the sink and washed them off. I glanced at the bedroom, then left the water running while I had a few words with Joe's fishing tackle: nothing fancy, but I knew he wouldn't be able to finish cleaning, so I talked it out of smelling so bad. When I got back, Joe pointed to an overstuffed manila folder on the dresser.

"Grab that, will you? Got to go over a few things. Most of what you need to know's in there, and the spare key's taped to the inside."

We went through it for a while. Mostly it

was little details, the sorts of things that need to be done to run a cemetery in New England where the ground freezes and you have to be damn careful with a plow. Phone numbers for a few guys who appreciated extra work. Where to find the records. Which signs to post about flowers and so on, and that he moved cut flowers and potted plants to the spot next to the Dumpster after a week or when they started to look wilted, and people were allowed to take them from there but not from the graves.

"You'll have to get one of those cellular phones, so they can get ahold of you. Answering machine's not good enough anymore, I suppose."

I grimaced.

"I know, I know," he said. "I can't stand them, either. But they only need to be able to get you until the ground's too frozen for that dinky backhoe. By Thanksgiving at the latest." After that, I already knew, anyone who died would have to be kept in cold storage until April or May.

"I understand," I said. "But what are the chances there'll be another burial this year anyway?"

His expression grew solemn. "One hundred

percent, Greg."

"One hundred percent?" I raised an eyebrow at him, prepared to chuckle at whatever joke he was getting ready to tell.

"Yuh. November fifth."

I caught myself and was glad not to still be balancing a plate on my knee. November fifth, 1981, was the day my brother went through the ice. It took me a second to remind myself that Joe wouldn't remember that. He must have picked the date out of thin air. I gave him a smile, as best I could to let him know I hadn't taken it amiss.

"You planning on killing someone, Joe? I'm not going to have to testify to anything, am I?"

He shook his head and threw me a dirty look. "There's always a body in Versailles on November fifth. Always. And always a young 'un. I know it sounds superstitious, but you've got the records—see for yourself."

"If that's true, shouldn't the police be involved?"

He looked surprised. "What? Why? It's accidents, Greg: car crashes, drownings, drunk hunters. Mostly young folks being stupid. It's just one of those things, nothing to worry over. But mark my word, there'll be a body on

November fifth, and with the weather this warm that means you've got to get a grave dug. All there is to it."

I HADN'T INTENDED TO LOOK into the November fifth thing. Sounded like a harmless joke, one that might have been fun for anyone else. But when I arrived at the graveyard and parked my car, the first grave marker I noticed—a handsome brass plaque set in a little granite slab—happened to say "5 Nov 1997." I saw another one on my way to the cottage on the grounds: a big old-fashioned stone from 1975, rounded on top and marked "Nov 5th" in tall, chiseled letters.

Stonewall Cemetery had been the town graveyard for about eighty years and had grown modestly during that time. I found the cottage, a squat little stone building which was really more of a shed, and then walked around a bit to try to get my bearings. I'd been there dozens of times, but always with someone else as guide: either to a grave site or a repair site. I kept seeing November fifths as I walked: 1984, 2004, 1960, 1995. Now, I'm aware that if he'd given any other date I'd have latched on to that instead. It's human nature. But he'd said November fifth, and it meant something to me, so that's what I fixated on.

From the far corner I could see my house, with all the lights on except the bedroom. I got grief for that sometimes, little comments about what my electric bill must be like. Nobody made a big deal of it, just the traditional Yankee way of saying, "We notice," and by extension, "We've got an eye on you." For the older folks it's a kind of lifeline, and for the younger folks it's a kind of jail. For me, it was complicated.

The truth of the electric bill was that on bright, sunny days I would unscrew all my light bulbs, bring them outside, and persuade them that *they* were the ones producing that nice bright light, not the sun. Then I'd take them all back indoors and screw them in: free light. A nicer light, too, I thought.

When I first got the idea, they lasted a day or so; lately they last about a month—or until I get forgetful (or someone thinks they're doing me a favor). The moment someone flips a light switch, the bulbs in that room go out. It doesn't matter what the switch is connected to, or even if it's connected at all: I once brought home a new GFCI switch from the hardware store and flipped it for no good reason while I carried it in, and all the lights in the living room went dark. I'm not sure why it happens, whether it's something in the bulb or something in the person, but out they all go. Annoys the piss out of me.

Having seen my house, I had a better sense of how the landscape was laid out. If that far corner was roughly northwest, then I could locate the main road even if I couldn't see it through the trees. Having oriented myself tolerably well, I made one last stop.

Adam's grave was visible from my yard, if you sat on the bench. The position of the bench was no accident, and neither was the location of the grave. My old dad had sat there with a binoculars to scout it out, while my mother murmured something about keeping his mind off things. Seventeen years old, Adam had been, only a little older than me. He'd been kinda loud, always grinning and confident; in a number of ways my opposite.

He had a knack for knowing the truth of things, too. I once lied to my old Honda skillfully enough to drive three miles on a bone-dry tank to arrive white-knuckled and hoarse at the Shell station, but I was never able to slip so much as a little white lie past Adam. Granted, I wasn't much good at it back then, and maybe I've built him up in my mind in the meantime, but I do think he had the opposite knack to mine.

I hunkered down in front of the marble stone and busied myself sweeping away brown and red leaves with my hands. *Adam Kellogg*, it read, *Beloved son and brother. Jul 7 1964 – Nov 5 1981*. I looked at the stone itself for a long time without thinking much of anything, but when I got ready to stand up, I noticed something odd. It looked like a charcoal smudge, down near the bottom, in the shape of an old-fashioned bomb: a sort of squared-off oval with fins. I knelt on the soft, cold ground and rubbed at it with my shirt sleeve, but it didn't come off. It wasn't paint, but it didn't look like part of the stone, either.

Without anything to clean it with anyway, I made my way back along the cemetery paths to the cottage. I saw another little bomb-shaped smudge on the back of an older-looking grave and wondered if some kid had a stencil and too much time.

Opening the cottage door brought the over-whelming smell of must and gasoline and dry clipped grass. There were two rooms. The first room, the biggest, had a barn door and was pretty much a garage for the lawn mower and the snow thrower. There were other tools: a gas-powered leaf blower and a Weedwacker hung from pegs on the wall alongside a couple rakes of different styles, shovels, clippers, and that kind of thing. Joe kept the place up well, and I had a feeling all the physical work kept him up well, too.

The second key got me into the office, which smelled faintly of gasoline and strongly of burned coffee. The offending item was a yellowed Mr. Coffee whose carafe hadn't been cleaned since... ever. I set to washing it in the little sink, using the cracked cake of hand soap since there wasn't any dish soap, and the dried coffee came off in flakes. I set it back on the burner wet rather than risk the rag hanging from the cabinet knob. I dumped out the grounds in the rubbish and discovered a half-second too late that there wasn't a liner in the bin.

I was looking for paper to make a shopping list when I found the map. It was on a big sheet of thick paper and looked liked it had been hand-copied from an older one—most of the layout and about half the numbers were all drawn in the same hand with similar dark black lines. The remaining layout was done in a narrower line width, and the accompanying numbers were all different colors and styles. Legible, all of it; there'd been care taken with it for many years. All the sections had numbers, and every grave had a section number and a grave number, like 5-14 for the fourteenth grave in section five.

Next to the map was an index. I'd known such a thing existed, but I always sort of figured it would be a big leather-bound tome inscribed with a quill pen. Instead, it was one of those college-ruled composition books with a black-and-white cover that looked like TV static, and lines on the front for Name and Grade. I flipped it open and leafed through. Someone had handwritten every single name, date of birth, date of death, and section and grave number since 1992. Blue pen, black pen, pencil. The writing changed in 1997, from someone's small, neat script to Joe's big, blocky penmanship and carefully written numbers with slashes through the sevens and little caps on the ones.

There were plenty of pages left; not all that many people died and were buried in Versailles. I found the last page, marked with a gas station receipt from 2003. That morning's funeral wasn't listed, so I'd have to see to that later. I flipped back a page, which was one whole year of deaths. My eye fell on the name Angela Westlake, Nov 5, grave 8-33. I looked for the previous Nov 5 and found Todd Boucher, and then David Thibault the Nov 5 before that.

There was a November fifth death every year through Joe's whole tenure, and then all the way back to the beginning. I checked each year off in my head as I went through again from the start, then closed the book and put it down. It was a strange piece of information. According to Joe, it was only a weird coincidence. I've never been great at math, but I figured it must be like the birthday thing: even though there's 365 days in a year, you only need two dozen people to be pretty sure there'll be at least one shared birthday. The odds of November fifth specifically being the day were astronomical, but the odds of there being such a day at all maybe weren't so bad?

It felt like I was lying to myself even though I was just mulling over half-remembered math, enough so that I forced myself to stop. A fella like me has to be careful about lying to himself, because you never know what'll happen. Hypochondriac liars don't live long, and deluding yourself about little things is a fine way to start down a dangerous road. There's a lot of stuff I don't let myself believe, even if it seems harmless to think there's an Easter bunny or that the new pastor who's so easy on the eyes appears to be finding excuses to drop by. The Stay Puft Marshmallow Man scene from Ghostbusters stuck in my head.

Fresh air would do me good, I decided, so I made my way back outside.

On opening the door, I smelled cigarette smoke: tobacco and cloves. In the time it took my brain to fish out the word "teenagers," they'd already heard the cottage door bang shut and made a run for it. Most of them had, anyway. Ashley Philips, Pastor Julie's daughter, remained. She stood with her arms crossed over her baggy sweatshirt, head tilted to one side as she inspected me. Her fingernails were painted black, and I wondered if that was new.

I looked toward her friends, who had already made it out the gates. "Do I smell bad?"

"They're just stupid." She didn't help me pick the smoldering cigarette butts out of the grass and stub them out on the gravel.

"Aren't they your friends?"

She shrugged. "You gonna tell my mom?"

"That your friends are stupid? She probably knows." I always had a feeling around Ashley that I was being subtly judged. This isn't all that unusual for me with teenagers, but she reminded me a little of Adam in that I felt a compulsion to see what kind of lie I could get away with.

She rolled her eyes. "You the new grave-digger now? I heard the old one fell in a grave and died."

"Sexton," I said. "It's like a gravedigger who gets to hire other people to do the digging. And Joe's all right, glad to say."

"That's good, I guess."

"It's good."

By that point in the conversation, such as it was, we had doubled the lifetime total number of words we'd ever said to each other. I decided to try for a record and walked over to a tall granite stone I'd noticed earlier with a November fifth death date. I had a feeling I knew what I'd see on the reverse side, and I called Ashley's attention to it.

"Since you're here," I said, "have you ever seen one of these markings before?"

She squinted. "Looks like a bomb."

"Yuh. I thought maybe one of the kids from school was doing it. Like a tag."

She gave me a look of withering scorn of the type only a full-blooded teenager can manage. "A 'tag'? Like, there's gangs in Versailles?" She put a strong emphasis on the "sails," and then made some inscrutable hand signal with fingers pointing every which way and stuck out her tongue. I thought I was going to be treated to another witticism when she tilted her head again and gave the symbol a second look, a real look this time.

"Is that paint?" she asked, finally.

"Dunno," I said. "I only noticed them to-day."

"Doesn't look like paint."

"Dunno," I repeated.

She glanced around and said dubiously, "There's another one over there."

"I've seen a few more. That's the funny thing," I said, thinking I might finally succeed in making some small connection with Pastor Julie's worrisome child. "So far, the only graves I've seen with it are for people who died on November fifth."

She gave me a wary look and took a step back.

"Creepy," she said. "I gotta go."

She ran off in the same direction her friends

had gone. I stood for awhile, thinking about not much in particular, and then glanced up to see a plane high in the sky overhead with a pair of contrails, and I knew where I'd seen something like that bomb thing before.

"IT CRASHED BACK IN THE forties, I think," I said to Pastor Julie while she ate her home fries with kind of a lot of ketchup. She'd asked for hot sauce to mix in, and Dotty, who owned the Polkadot Diner, just laughed and said that sounded interesting and she'd have to get some. Dotty said that every time Pastor Julie asked but none had appeared. I wasn't entirely sure Dotty knew what hot sauce was.

"And it had those bomb markings on it?"

I nodded. "To tally up bombing runs. It's a while since I was last up there, but I seem to remember they looked like that."

Dotty brought me a nice thick slice of blueberry pie and refilled my coffee while she was there. Damn good coffee Dotty makes, more than reason enough to forgive her the hot sauce thing.

"Greg Kellogg," Pastor Julie said, "Super Yankee." I smiled and nodded as a kind of bow. When we'd first met, the year before when she moved to Versailles from Boston, I'd told her about E. B. White's Yankee Hierarchy. It starts off pointing out that to foreigners, a "Yankee" is any old American, then winds through the country with everybody defining somebody else as a "Yankee," ending up with the New Englanders pointing at Vermonters, and Vermonters, stuck in a corner, pointing at those folks who have pie for breakfast. Or maybe it's folks who still use outhouses; I forget.

Anyhow. As it happens, I like to have pie for breakfast, and had mentioned at some point that I'd lived in Vermont while I was at college, so Pastor Julie called me "Super Yankee" whenever we happened to have breakfast together. And we're always there after the earlier-than-thou crowd clears out so nobody hears her say it, and that is fine by me.

I'd called her the evening before to accept the sexton job, and she insisted on taking me out to breakfast—not "brunch"—so we could cover what she needed from me and make sure I had what I needed to do the job. All that had been taken care of by the time I'd finished my first coffee, so I'd filled the time telling her about the markings I'd seen on the graves, and my theory about where the symbol had come from. She tasted her scrambled eggs, and as she added salt, said, "So you think some local kids saw it on the wreck and picked it up as an emblem or something?"

"I don't know. I can't tell if it's paint or a chemical stain or crayon wax or what. I called Joe, but he didn't seem to know what I was talking about."

We ate in silence for a while, and I'm pretty sure Pastor Julie finished off the ketchup bottle. Dotty refilled my coffee again even though I said I was fine, since she and I both knew I'd drink it anyway.

"It seems to me," Pastor Julie said, staring down at her plate, "that if it's a prank, some work went into it. You said you saw the mark on a grave from last November. The headstones go up, what, a few months after burial? So, less than a year since the last one could have been done, and you counted a dozen until you got bored. That's a lot of graves to track down and mark without getting caught. And why November fifth? Do people celebrate Guy Fawkes Day up here?"

I explained the strange coincidence of a death occurring every year on that date, to her obvious and growing incredulity.

"No! Really?" She squinted at me like she was trying to tell if I was pulling a fast one. "*Really?*"

"Really. I looked it up in the grave list myself. One every year, back at least as far as the nineties. I've been wondering why nobody noticed it, but Joe did. The police, too, I expect. Maybe someone else did, and this is their way of commemorating the occasion."

"Like, you've flipped a coin heads a dozen times in a row, so you cheer on every new one?"

"I don't know about *cheering*," I said. I didn't have any pie left, so I pushed around the blueberry smear with my fork a bit. "Doesn't feel like cheering. Maybe superstition. Maybe someone's trying to get it to stop."

Dotty brought the bills, one for each of us, and we both paid cash. She takes checks from locals but I know it's a pain for her, and anyway she prefers cash. Pastor Julie always tipped well, I noticed, even though the church probably didn't pay much.

"I'm free until one," she said. "If you have time, I'd kinda like to see that plane."

I'D BEEN TO THE CRASH site a couple times since I was young. It's a nice hike up the northern slope, though cold that time of year thanks to not getting much sun. Halfway up the trail there's a cell phone tower, idiotically disguised as a pine tree. A *California* pine tree. It sticks out more than a plain green pole would, and they tell me it collects more bird shit than any other tree in the forest. That last part's not true, of course, but I think it's funny and I repeat it whenever I get the chance.

We chatted on the way up, Pastor Julie and me, I think partly to prove to each other that we weren't winded by the climb. Nothing of consequence, just complaining about how the leaf peepers jammed up the roads and whether it was going to snow anytime soon. Truth be told, it's an easy trail, and when we came upon an older couple coming downhill, we didn't even have to move much out of the way for them. Even so, I may have told myself a few times that I had plenty of energy and didn't need a breather, and as true as that was, let's say it doesn't always occur to me to call my attention to the fact.

"Beautiful view," Pastor Julie said when we came to the first clearing, where the old fire tower used to be. I sat down on a rock and may have given my shoes a glance that implied I thought I might need to retie them. She started for the space next to me and I scooted over to make room, but she wandered toward the ledge instead. "I should bring Ashley up here. It's good exercise."

"Yup." We were quiet for a while, taking in the view. "How're things at the church?"

Her eyes saddened. "Oh, everything's all right. It's getting toward our busy season, but at least I have a month before the Christmas preparations."

That wasn't really what I was asking; I was more wondering if she was still getting pushback or feeling unwelcome. In an unguarded moment a few weeks ago she had vented a little that she "wasn't getting through" to a lot of the older folks. She hadn't said anything since, but that look in her eyes right then made me think things hadn't improved.

"I'm getting cold," she said suddenly, and marched past me up the mountain.

It wasn't far from there to the first piece of the wreck, part of a wing. It was big, at least eight feet long and close enough to the main trail to be covered with graffiti. Neither engine was attached; I was under the impression that the Army Air Corps had hauled them out so that German spies couldn't get a look at them. And I dimly remembered being told as a kid that a German spy had been caught in town back during the war. Or maybe he was Russian. Either way, there was a grave site down the hill that all the kids called the Spy's Tomb, where the younger kids went to tell each other ghost stories and the older kids to have sex.

We stood and gawked at it for a little while, then Pastor Julie took a picture with her phone and we made for the steeper left-hand trail that led to the fuselage. It was a B-17 bomber that had survived Black Thursday and the trip across the Atlantic, just to crash into a damn mountain.

The bomber's altimeter had malfunctioned during an early blizzard, our scoutmaster had told us, and it plowed into the rock face. No survivors, though I've heard tell of people surviving crashes even worse than that. The Army picked it clean of anything sensitive once the snow let up, of course, but there was still the wreckage of the fuselage, parts of the wings and tail, and a lot of scrap.

It didn't take long to find the piece I remembered. The cockpit glass itself was long since shattered and buried by hikers' feet and weather, but under where it had been were a dozen black stencil marks, visible even after long years and harsh winters. Bombs, like the one I'd seen on Adam's grave and the others.

"Wow," Pastor Julie said. "I've never seen a crashed plane before. That's amazing."

I said something by way of agreement and continued up the trail to get a better look at the stencils. The trail led around the larger pieces— or rather, a parade of curious hikers had managed to stomp a trail over the years—and we got a good look at the various twisted metal bits that had been left behind. The front of the plane and the cockpit instruments had been demolished, first by the crash and then by a fire, but the rest of the wreck was at least recognizable as having been a plane.

On a whim, I'd grabbed the tape measure from my toolkit; I put it to use then and found all the stencils to be four and a half inches tall by two inches wide, with the little triangular fins about an inch. I jotted the figures down on my notepad.

Pastor Julie was giving me an amused look. I shrugged. "I'm curious about our vandal's attention to detail, I guess." That wasn't entirely true; something was bothering me. Not any particular thing, just a kind of feeling. As I finished speaking, I felt a cold breeze off the mountain.

"Well, how do they stack up?"

They were an exact match, but I felt a little hesitant to discuss it right there. "Oh, I'll need to measure the ones back at the graveyard." The wind picked up, and I wrapped my arms around myself and stamped my feet. My climbing partner didn't look too affected, but she'd dressed a little more wisely for the trip than I had.

"So," she said, "you mentioned that you do a lot of hiking. Do you come up here much?"

"Maybe once or twice a year," I said. "Mostly I take the eastern trail. Most people do, I guess. It's a nicer hike."

"You hike by yourself a lot?" She ran a gloved hand along the edge of a metal something-or-other with faded blue paint on it.

"Pretty much always."

She looked straight at me. "Do you ever wish you spent less time alone?"

"Oh, um… It's not so bad," I found myself stammering out.

Pastor Julie's phone started singing the "Song of the Volga Boatmen" just then. She sighed. "The school," she said, then pulled her glove off with her teeth and walked back down the trail a bit to answer the call.

I wandered off to let her have her privacy, gawking at twisted aluminum and long-rotted leather. With no scoutmaster to stop me, I left the trail and wandered through the thick frosted leaves to get a look at the other side.

The far side of the fuselage, partly buried in earth and leaves, was shielded from the sun and covered in frost. I saw dark blobs under the ice crystals, and when I rubbed at the top where the frost was lightest, I saw more black bombs. At least another dozen.

I glanced up at Pastor Julie, who was pacing as she talked, with that slab of a phone cradled against her head. She wasn't paying any attention to me, so I knelt down and whispered to the aluminum. "Amazing how warm it is," I had started saying when I was interrupted by the wind picking up with a howling vengeance. It chilled me to the bone and I couldn't wrap my jacket around myself tight enough, but the cold wasn't what bothered me. No, it was the crazy idea that, in the middle of the frigid howl, someone had said something, or rather snarled it.

"That was the wind," I told myself, but didn't believe it even enough to be worth reprimanding myself for wishful thinking.

She came back with her phone pressed to one ear and three fingers over the microphone.

"I have to go," she said with an apologetic look. "I'll give you a lift back if you want to come now."

I absolutely did.

Still distracted by what I'd heard, or *thought* I'd heard, I stumbled along behind her. I would have sworn the wind had been a whispering voice, angry and cold. I would also have sworn that its single word had been: *Liar!*

I LEARNED TO LIE—IN THE interesting sense, I mean—from a college professor who used to summer here in Versailles. Henry Myers came up to town every June and left every August for a dozen years or so, and had been working on a textbook about the philosophy of argument that whole time. In retrospect it was obvious that he'd recognized in me someone with his own skills. Lies like we tell—my light bulbs, Henry's fishing lures—everything we ply our craft on has a sense of suspension about it. It's hard to put it better than that, but it's a feeling of expectation, of gravity holding its breath while waiting for Wile E. Coyote to look down.

Now, Henry had told me that he'd realized my ability when I helped him fix a flat one day for five bucks, but he'd been coming to town long before then, and I think now that he'd set it up as a test.

Henry was a weird old bird. He called himself a persuader, and I tried not to call our craft 'lying' in his presence because he didn't like it. He was a mid-westerner, from Minnesota, and got along with New Englanders just fine. He talked about politics only sparingly, though he listened to NHPR all the time (back when it was Granite State Public Radio) and made all manner of snorting, scoffing, and hooting noises when politicians came on.

Later on he bequeathed his unfinished textbook to me in his will, after succumbing to late stage cancer. He'd managed to persuade himself that he would die of it, and by golly he did, and I never did know whether his knowledge of his manner of death was descriptive or prescriptive.

I found myself thinking about old Henry as we got to the trailhead, walking in silence. He'd impressed upon me the importance of trusting my senses. "Don't fool yourself, Greg," he used to warn me. "If you don't perceive clearly, your persuasions will do more harm than good. It's like building on sand." I let that memory float around inside my head a bit without recognizing whether it attached to any particular experience.

I got into Pastor Julie's truck—we'd car-pooled from the Polkadot—still quiet. She put her hands on the wheel without starting the ignition.

"I don't know what I'm going to do about her, Greg." She stared straight ahead like she was driving. "Skipping class. Drinking. Is this normal misbehaving? Should I be worried about her? I expected some of this—it's a new town and she's the pastor's daughter, there's a lot of temptation to act out. I just…"

She made an inarticulate noise, slammed her left palm on the steering wheel, and turned the key. It took a moment for the engine to turn over, then we were on our way. It was only a couple minutes' drive around the southeast corner of town, but it was nice to be off our feet.

"She's not a bad kid," Pastor Julie said as we drove. "I don't think there really is such a thing as a bad kid, or a bad anybody. Only people."

"People can be frustrating," I offered.

"They sure as—" I detected the hint of a

"sh" on the tip of her tongue. She had not been a pastor long and sometimes had trouble playing the part. "They sure are."

We turned into the little lot next to the Polkadot Diner, the gravel crunching under her heavy truck's wheels.

"Thanks for listening," she said as she pulled up to my Honda. "I appreciate that there's someone here who I can vent to without getting an earful of advice."

I was glad she took my cluelessness as politeness. "Any time," I said.

She smiled. "You know the best part, Greg? You really mean that."

WHEN I GOT HOME LATER that evening after a repair job at the volunteer fire department, there was a message on the answering machine from my mother, wanting to know my Thanksgiving plans. It wasn't an invitation, since I had no interest in flying to Florida nor they in flying back here. Just a general desire to know that I wasn't planning to sit alone in the dark, weeping over a can of cold cat food. Seven years ago I'd joked about that and she's called out of concern every year since.

I called her back after dinner and we chatted

for a little while. I deflected her questions about that "nice lady pastor" and she was vague when I asked if she was still letting Dad drive, and it was pretty much like every other conversation we ever had.

"How awful for Joe," she said after I filled her in on the job at the cemetery. "Tell him we're sending our regards and best wishes."

"Will do. Any suggestions for taking care of the place?"

"Well," she said after a pause, "I don't know much about cemeteries. You're already keeping up the family graves—and thank you for that, dear. Do the kids still hang out near the Spy's Tomb?"

"I don't know. Is it really a spy buried there?"

She laughed. "I'm sure it isn't. Some poor hobo, probably. That was before my time, during the war. I think it was the older kids who called it that. Your Aunt Cheryl and I once took a Ouija board out there, did I ever tell you that? She tried to scare me with it, the stinker."

We shared a laugh, then got off on a tangent about Cheryl's hip surgery and whether she still had the Ouija board.

"Oh, Mom, before I forget," I said, laying

on the casualness maybe a little thick. "When you and Dad lived here, do you ever remember seeing these little bomb stencils around town?"

"Bombs? Well, Gregory, what a thought! You mean black-balls-with-fuses kind of things?"

"More like World War Two, those big oval shapes like they stenciled on planes."

"Oh, like Adam used to doodle? No, I don't think so."

She may have gone on a bit longer but I had stopped paying attention. I didn't remember Adam drawing anything like that, but I was on the cordless phone (which is not an Infernal Device as it stays at home), so I went upstairs to the room where Adam's things were kept in boxes, alongside some stuff my parents had left behind. It's not a shrine or anything, I just don't like to throw things out that they maybe might want someday.

Saying "uh-huh" and "sure" at appropriate intervals, I opened the top box, which was marked "ADAM DESK/SCHOOOL" in Magic Marker, possibly aided by a glass of wine. I bent and opened the flaps, which had been folded over each other instead of taped, and pulled out his old blue-and-white Trapper Keeper. We'd each received one as a gift from our grandparents, who had never quite gotten the hang of the cookies-and-candy thing.

"Well, it's been good talking to you, Greg, but I need to go. Maureen's coming over to help with the Halloween decorations."

"Uh-huh," I said. "Sure. Say hi to Dad."

I'd already opened the brittle PVC folder and found the blue-lined pages inside, which had gotten yellowed over the years. The first folder's papers were all marked "1979" at the top. I flipped past the folders to the half-inch stack of loose paper, and after some leafing through, there it was: shaded in pencil on a page of algebra notes dated "Oct 28." It was a half-hearted thing, not even filled in all the way, but a recognizable bomb shape nonetheless. On the next page they were in the margins, and kinda looked like fat vertical ichthus fish. More on Monday the second, and still more the days after until his notes from the fourth had together about a dozen of the things. The fifth had been a snow day, thanks to a burst pipe, and Adam had died that afternoon.

Although I vividly remembered Adam going through the ice, I recalled very little else about that time, let alone whether my older brother had said anything about bombs or gone to visit the crash site. My mother spent a lot of time in Adam's room afterward, collecting his school-work and other things together. I could picture her sitting there, the door half-closed. Of course she remembered the little drawings, she just hadn't realized that he'd only started doing them a few days before he died.

Adam had been so sure that the ice was safe to walk on, and with reason: he had a knack for knowing the truth of things like that; the way I could persuade a truck bumper to be sturdy, he invariably knew whether it would fall off if he climbed on it. I could fool the universe and sometimes my parents, but never Adam. That day on the ice was the only time I'd ever known him to be wrong.

GINI LEVESQUE, THE TOWN LIBRARIAN, was always gracious when I stopped by on my own, because it meant she could put me to work on something or other without worrying about imposing. I never charged the library or the police for my services, only for parts, and she always felt a little uncomfortable asking me to come in. So by the time I arrived that morning, the bubbler's drain had probably been clogged for a week. Leaned against the nozzle was a neat hand-printed index card reading "Out of Order" which had plainly been soaked and air-dried a couple times.

I got my toolkit from in front of my Honda's passenger seat and took the front cover off the plumbing. Once Gini went back to the front desk, I talked the clog into washing itself down the drain, tapped at the pipe a few times for verisimilitude, and then had a drink of cold water. Drain was clear as a whistle.

By the time I was done, Gini had pulled down the obituaries binders, mostly clipped from the *Berlin Daily Sun* and kept around for genealogists. She'd already heard that I was taking over as cemetery caretaker, and I let her put two and two together to get whatever she wanted.

It took me a while to figure out what I was looking for, since I'd gone to the library on impulse more than anything. But after an hour and a half, I had a pretty good idea of things. First, the November fifth deaths went back at least to 1971, the earliest binder Gini had found; one every year, always someone under twenty-one. The youngest was fifteen. In 1973 there were three on the same day, a car crash. Dozens over the years, all told. I didn't remember much statistics, but that sounded damned unlikely to me.

That part was easy. It was the second bit that took some time, since I had to read a few unrelated obituaries to notice it: while most obituaries didn't list a cause of death, none of the November fifth ones mentioned illness or suggested donations to the American Cancer Society. Some had articles paperclipped to them about car accidents, or a tree blown down in a gale, but most were hazy on the subject or just said "accidental."

I brought the binders back up to the desk and thanked Gini. Casually I added, "I was up hiking near the old crashed plane yesterday. You ever been up there?"

"Once, when I was a little girl." She frowned. "It gave me the willies. Why?"

"Oh, I was just wondering what you knew about it."

"Well!" She cleared her throat. "The plane was a B-17 Flying Fortress that was damaged in a raid over Schweinfurt, Germany, in 1943. It was on its way to Rome, New York, with a crew of seven when it was caught in a blizzard. The altimeter malfunctioned and the plane crashed with no survivors. The Army came after the snow lifted and recovered some equipment but had to leave most of the wreck intact." She smiled. "Is that what you wanted to know?"

I nodded appreciatively. I asked even though I was sure of the answer. "Do you recall when the crash was?"

"But of course! November third, 1943. Er, Greg? Is something wrong?"

I FORMED AND DISCARDED A dozen theories on the short drive over to Doug's Marketplace, the only grocery store in town. The first to be discarded was that Gini was misremembering the date, because Gini never misremembered anything. Just ask her husband.

Second to go was the notion that there was no link. I was a liar, and a damned good one, and I knew the smell of my own brand of falsehood. There was something not right about the whole business, something that unsettled me, and it wasn't just the idea that Adam was involved. Though, if I were being honest with myself, that was a lot of it. Anyhow, the "no link" theory was out.

There was plenty that could have happened between November third, 1943, and November fifth, 1971, though. Maybe Guy Fawkes Day *was* thrown in there somehow. Anyway, Gini was on the hunt for obituaries for me to see where the run started. That might narrow things down, but I kinda wanted to figure it out on my own. I felt this was a problem that could be solved somehow, and that I was the guy to do it.

I picked up flour, sugar, butter, and a sack of Braeburns to go with the Granny Smiths at home. On impulse I grabbed a bottle of merlot, too. Doug's only stocked three varieties of wine, two of which were plonk, but the merlot was pretty good. It had occurred to me once or twice to see if I could improve it, but lying to food was a very bad idea.

There aren't many aisles in Doug's, but wandering them gave me enough time to think over what little I knew. Someone, usually a teenager, died in Versailles every November fifth. Forty-odd accidental deaths, one a year on the same day. At *least* one, I corrected myself, remembering the car crash. Their graves in Stonewall Cemetery had been marked with the same bomb emblem as a WWII bomber that had crashed around the same time of year in 1943. Adam had become… my brain reached for "obsessed" but I corrected myself. Adam had become *interested* in the symbol in the days before his own death. And Adam had died, I believed, because his knack for knowing the truth of things, his ever-fresh and always-justified confidence, had failed him.

Joe had been sure there would be another death on the fifth, and now so was I. But Joe had accepted it as just one of those things, while I was afraid it was something worse.

"Everything all right, Greg?" Kenny gave me an odd look when I got to the register. He was Doug's son, Doug himself having passed away years ago. "You look like your dog died."

I made small talk but my heart wasn't in it. No, nothing wrong. No, not getting Halloween candy since the kids never climbed the hill to my house. Et cetera. I paid the bill and put the bags on the front passenger seat. The wine was kinda rolling around and I was afraid it would fall onto my tools, so I put it in the glove box and told it a quick lie to keep shut.

I WAS STANDING AT THE island in my kitchen with my elbows on the counter and a recipe printout in front of me when the phone rang. It was Pastor Julie, and she sounded frantic.

"Greg, is Ashley there?"

I blinked. "No. Why—should she be?"

"No. I don't know, I just—she's missing. She disobeyed me and went out to Berlin with her friends but now they're back and she's not and they said they dropped her off near the cemetery but she's not there." That all came out in one breath and she had to stop for a second when she was done. At the mention of the cemetery, I felt a chill. It wasn't quite November, not for a few hours, but she and her friends were about the right age. And anyway, angry ghosts aren't the only known killers of teenagers. Probably not even in the top ten.

"All right," I said. "I'm sure there's nothing to worry about. Have you called the police?"

"They said they'd keep an eye out, but they've got their hands full with trick-or-treating, and they said she's probably with her friends. Different friends. I don't know."

I reached back and turned off the preheating oven. "Give me a minute, I'll come help you look."

"No, that's all right. I'm going to drive around, so I left her a note on the door that if she can't get ahold of me, she should call you. And you have a phone book, in case I need a number for one of her friends' parents. Just be there, OK?"

"OK. Sure. I'm here if you need me."

There was silence on the line. Then: "Thanks, Greg."

I stood with the phone in my hands for a while before putting it back on its base. Something about Ashley and the cemetery bothered me. I went outside and walked across the yard to where I could see flashlights in the streets and peered down at the graveyard. No lights there, anyway.

After a while, I came back to the house so I'd hear the phone ring, and eventually decided I might as well start the pie after all. That had been a pretty good way of inviting a distraction lately. I turned the oven back on, then looked for the merlot but couldn't remember where I'd put it, so I cracked open a Sam Adams instead.

The recipe called for precooking the filling, so I peeled and sliced the apples and put them in a cast-iron pan with some cinnamon and nutmeg and cloves, and a cup of sugar. I took the soaked raisins from the fridge and stirred them in. It smelled nice, and the phone didn't ring. I turned on NPR and hummed along with the evening jazz program as I rolled out the crust, folded it in half and then half again on some plastic wrap, and put it back in the fridge.

The filling was about cooked when the doorbell rang. I frowned at it. The house hadn't gotten trick-or-treaters in twenty years. Pastor Julie usually called before she came over; a glance told me that the phone was on the hook, but she might have forgot and tried the Infernal Device instead. I wiped the flour off my hands and answered the front door. There on the step, dressed like a kind of pirate, I guess, and holding her arms like she was shivering, was Ashley.

"Come in," I didn't get a chance to say before she squeezed past me.

"*Oh my God*, it's so *cold* out there."

"Where's your coat?" I asked, and got a withering glare in reply. "Well, it's warm in the kitchen. Come on in."

I shut the door and ushered her inside. She rubbed her bare arms as she preceded me into the kitchen and seated herself on one of the tall chairs around the island.

"Can I get you—" I caught myself before offering her "a drink." "A cup of coffee or cocoa or something?"

"Coffee," she said, in a muted voice because her chin was tucked down onto her chest.

I opened the dry sink's upper cabinet to get at the Keurig machine, last year's birthday gift from my parents. It's not that I'm embarrassed to own one, I just think it looks better when you can't see it. I gave her the box of K-cups while it shuddered and groaned and gurgled. She picked a flavored one, hazelnut, which I don't drink, but they came in a mix pack and it would be wasteful to throw them out. I was careful not to be judgmental as I inserted it into the machine and put a plain white mug under it.

"What are you making?" she asked. "Applesauce?"

"Apple pie," I said. "I'm experimenting to see if I can get it the way I like it."

"I don't know how to make pie," she said. "My mom doesn't bake, except bread for *church*."

"Well, watch and learn," I said. The Keurig was ready, so I closed the lid and pushed the button. A minute later, I handed her the steaming mug of black coffee, and then the creamer and sugar as she requested them.

I glanced at the phone on the side table and decided to use the one upstairs to call Pastor Julie. While Ashley stirred her coffee, I murmured, "Just using the bathroom, I'll be back in a second."

"If you call my mom, I'll be gone before you

hang up," she said. There wasn't any emotion in it, she said it matter-of-factly. I stopped.

"I wasn't—"

"I can tell when you're lying," she said in the same flat tone. "I can tell when everyone's lying. So don't bother."

I stared at her. She could have been quoting Adam, word for word. Not bravado, but simple confidence and statement of fact. She stared into her coffee, then tasted it.

"I'm hoping," I said, choosing my words with care, "to do what's best for you and your mom."

"Hope springs eternal," she said, pouring sugar straight from the bowl instead of using her wet spoon. "Whatever that means."

"If you know when I'm lying, you know that was the truth."

"Everyone *means* well. They're usually just stupid and wrong."

I wondered if emailing would work, since that wasn't calling, but suspected it wouldn't. Anyway, the computer was off—I always turn it off before I drink so I'm not tempted to edit Wikipedia.

"So why did you come up here? I mean, I'm glad for the company," I added without thinking. I wasn't sure whether that was completely true, but she let it pass.

"It was that or freeze to death. Besides, you're all right when you're not hitting on my mom."

I replied automatically: "I'm not—"

She fixed me with a glare that only a teenager in her prime can muster, and I let it go. The timer for the apples went off.

"She's out driving around looking for you right now," I said, extinguishing the gas flame under the pan. "Seems a little cruel to let her keep doing it."

She slurped her coffee and appeared to mull it over. "How about I text her and let her know I'm OK, and then you don't have to call."

That sounded reasonable, so I agreed. She pulled from her little bag a phone that looked like the monolith from that movie *2001* and started tapping at it. Then she went back to her coffee.

"Well, since you're here," I said, "why don't you help me finish the pie? I hope you'll let me call your mom when we're done, but we can cross that bridge when we get to it, all right?"

I'd turned off the burner but the cast-iron pan full of apples was still hot. Ordinarily, I'd have persuaded it that its handle was cool enough to touch, but I didn't want an audience for that trick. Instead I got out the welding glove I use for a potholder and moved the pan to a trivet on the island.

She peered at the apples and raisins and took a long whiff. Her phone made a little yipping noise like a chihuahua, but she ignored it. "Ew, raisins."

"They're good," I said. "They mix up the texture so it's not the same all the way through."

"Yeah, but if it's good, it's OK if it's the same all the way through. Why would you want to mix it up unless it sucks?"

I scratched my chin for a minute. I didn't have an answer to that. "Too much of a good thing, I suppose."

"Nobody makes you take a ginormous slice."

This was true. "I soaked the raisins in spiced rum for an hour."

She nodded sagely. "Good answer."

With Ashley's help, I got the bottom piecrust into the blue ceramic pie plate and let her dock the bottom—or as she put it, "go psycho with a fork."

"What do you think?" I said. "Blind bake the crust?"

She gave me a blank look.

"Put the empty crust in the oven now so it cooks and browns, then take it back out again to fill it with the apples. The recipe says no, but I think it might work better."

Ashley put her elbows up on the island and her head in her hands, and appeared to think deeply. She shook her head. "Go with the recipe."

"All right." I pulled on the welding glove and held the cast-iron pan over the bottom crust while she scooped out the cooked filling. "Be careful," I said as I saw her sneaking a black-nailed finger toward it. "That stuff's napalm."

I handed her a spatula from the jar and left her to spread out the precooked apples and raisins and pat them down while I rolled out the top crust. The smells of cinnamon and applesauce got a lot stronger as she stirred. I caught myself before admonishing her not to tear the bottom of the crust. All told, it wasn't the worst thing that could happen, and I was starting to get an inkling that she didn't spend a lot of time between corrections.

Other than the occasional "Hand me that, please," we worked in quiet. She didn't appear to be in the mood to talk, and I don't really know what to say to teenage girls.

We laid the top crust on together, and it went on well centered and without tearing, for which we congratulated each other solemnly. We trimmed and crimped the edges, and then I slashed the pastry with my paring knife to let the steam out. The recipe called for coarse sugar on top, but I don't like that, so I just did the egg wash. I opened the preheated oven and braved the wave of hot air to gently lower the pie onto the rack, holding it gingerly by the lip of the plate so as not to ruin the nice crimped edge.

"Are you screwing my mom?"

I fumbled only for a second, but it was enough: the pie slipped out of my right hand and flipped over onto the rack. Apples poured through the holes in the top crust, which opened obscenely to pass them in a heap onto the hot oven floor. They sizzled and a cloud of steam billowed, followed by black smoke and the stench of burning sugar.

Ashley burst out laughing.

I turned off the oven and made for the windows, which I opened at the top as wide as I could. Her laughing turned to coughing as smoke filled the room. The smoke alarm went off, which set her laughing again as she fled the room.

This was not my first burned pie, and I was prepared. I ducked down into the root cellar and found the box fan where I'd left it. It went snugly into the window, and after I pulled cobwebs off the plug and turned it on, it did a good job. The smoke started to clear pretty much right away.

Even with the oven off and open, the filling kept burning. It was black and bubbling by now, and I could already picture the long, hard scraping it would take to clean up.

"You don't seem so hot to me," I mumbled, very *very* quietly. Behind me I heard the front door open, probably Ashley airing the house. "Looks like the apples just took the heat right out and cooled things down. See, the smoke's already going away. Like quenching a horse-shoe. Why, I bet I could stick my finger on it, no problem."

"What in the *Hell* is going on here?" When Pastor Julie said "Hell" you heard the capital "H."

I didn't hear my finger sizzle on the bottom of the stove as I lost my concentration but I sure felt it. I jumped and whacked my head on the top of the oven so hard the whole box jumped. "Shit!"

"It's not what it looks like, Mom!"

I shook my head to clear it, even though that doesn't do any good, and stuck my finger in my mouth. Pastor Julie was standing in my living room, looking into my kitchen, and she wore on her face an expression of fury I'd never seen before or since.

Ashley stood between us, facing her mother, and for some reason she had taken half her clothes off. Pastor Julie looked about ready to burn my house down. For my own part, I was staring at Ashley, dumbfounded. Not for the obvious reason, though: down in the small of her bared back was a little black tattoo surrounded by angry red skin and covered with clear peeling plastic. It was in the shape of a bomb.

"'Shit!' is right, Greg." Pastor Julie's voice was hoarse and her face bright red. "Get in the car, Ashley."

"Mom—"

"Car. Get in. The car."

Ashley, holding her shirt up in front of her with her brassiere dangling from one hand, dashed into the kitchen, grabbed her bag, and zipped right on past her mother and outside. I only saw her expression for a moment but she looked exceptionally pleased with herself.

"I can't believe you, Greg. I can't *believe* you. When I told you she was misbehaving, it wasn't a fucking *invitation*." Her voice cracked.

"I was just making a pie—"

"See what happens when you get distracted? Was she up here when I called, Greg? When I was frantic looking for her? Were you—Augh!" She cut herself off and made a disgusted face.

"It's not like that—"

"Liar!" Her voice outright broke.

She tried to slam the front door behind her on her way out, but it bounced and swung open again. I heard her truck start, and gravel pelted the house as she peeled away.

Well, shit.

IT TOOK ME MORE THAN a few minutes to pull myself together after all that. But I rallied sufficiently to talk the oven down to a temperature cool enough to scrape the burned apples and pie-crust scraps off the bottom. Good, hard manual labor has a beneficial effect on the mental processes, as my grandfather used to say.

I did not for one moment believe Ashley had picked that tattoo at random. I had a strong feeling she knew what it meant, in the same way that I think Adam knew it, too, and maybe even knew what it meant for him.

It occurred to me that if the tattoo foretold what I thought it did, maybe a pretty big obstacle would be removed for me in five days.

I went back to the good, hard manual labor, as after that unworthy thought my mental processes obviously needed some additional beneficial effect. I put my back into it, and some hot water from the kettle, and spent a good half-hour scrubbing. My arms ached and my back ached and my hands were raw, but my head was clear. I didn't know what the connection was between the November third plane crash and the November fifth deaths, but there was one. Something would have to be done, and I figured I was the guy to do it.

THE TRIP UP THE MOUNTAINSIDE isn't any easier after dark, but I had one of those headlamps and I knew the way pretty well. Even so, I felt like my feet found every loose root and stone on the entire trail. My ankles hurt and my knees hurt and it took me a good fifteen minutes longer than it should have, but eventually I made my way up to the crash site.

I could tell before I saw the plane that it was

nearby: cold radiated off the twisted metal and I felt a keen sense that I was intruding. Under ordinary circumstances I might liken it to walking in on a private conversation, but I felt instead as if I'd gotten between a dog and its bowl.

Keeping my distance from the bulk of the wreck, I slid off my backpack and opened it. I'd taken a few lightbulbs from my living room and wrapped them in socks; I knew enough not to look directly at them, but I was still blinded for a minute when I unwrapped the first one. I felt with my hands for a soft spot of mulched leaves and moss to set it down.

I had an overwhelming feeling of exposure as I did that. Anyone below could see it, and I wouldn't be surprised if someone called in a fire alarm. I'd prepared a story for that and brought along my big bright lantern. The battery was dead, or I'd have used it on the climb up, but it would let me explain that I'd been up here a few days ago and dropped the Infernal Device, which was in my pocket. Assuming Pastor Julie ever spoke to me again, she could corroborate at least that part of the story.

The wind picked up, obliging me to pull my coat tight.

I had a little experience undoing lies other than my own. There's not really a trick to it, it's more like unraveling a tightly knotted shoelace: you pull here, you dig in there, and you pay attention to where you're making headway so you know where to concentrate. Henry had taught me how to do it because he was curious whether the skill could be passed on. His "persuasions" had been a hell of a lot stronger than mine at the time, to the point where he could sort of weld metal. He didn't do it with heat, but by persuading the two pieces of metal that they already were stuck together. One day he had me take off a plate he'd "welded" to his muffler; it was in the wrong spot so he'd have to do it anyway, which knowledge had been helpful in persuading it that it wasn't really stuck on there at all, because who would have done something so foolish? Henry hadn't *appreciated* my approach, but it had worked.

"There's not really any such thing as ghosts," I said aloud, conversationally. "I don't know where people got the idea."

The cold changed; it wasn't so much a feeling of frigid air anymore as that the temperature of everything was dropping, myself included. Whatever was out there to give its attention to me, I had it. But it was not real, not the truth. An angry spirit is a lie. And a lie can be undone.

"Now, if you think about it," I continued, "they can't possibly be real. On the one hand, there's this idea of a crazy angry ghost that kills one person a year and leaves a calling card. Pretty spooky, but it doesn't make sense. There's no reason for the dead to resent the living, that's just silly. It's *seventy years* since this plane crashed, for crying out loud."

I went on in that vein for a while to warm myself up, then changed tack. There's an art to the kind of circular argument I had decided on. The bigger the lie, the gentler it has to go. But the gist of it was: if there were a ghost, why would I be there on Halloween? Nobody would do that, especially not in New England. But I did do that, so there must not be a ghost. And if there are no ghosts, then the November fifth deaths were all random, like a coin coming up heads a lot of times in a row. There was no more reason for anyone to die in five days than on any other day of the year, and the odds against Ashley specifically dying on that day were astronomical.

"A lie implies a liar," Henry said once, and teenage me had thought that was deep.

Thinking about it on the drive up, I'd decided it was the key. Lies like I tell can come from one good liar but also a lot of subconscious ones, and New Englanders have always been fond of a certain type of story. The first few deaths were probably real accidents. Someone noticed and connected them to the crash—just because Gini knew the right date doesn't mean everybody did. After that, collective superstition got things rolling, and a succession of cemetery caretakers and who knows who else kept it going.

It grew colder as I talked, and the wind rose and fell. I made a remark once or twice about the perfectly natural chill and tied that into my argument. I was going with a kind of wall-of-speech approach, though it has some downsides, one of which is that I can't know whether it's worked until I stop. But I figured that didn't hurt, since I wouldn't know until November fifth whether it worked anyway.

I had a good head of steam going into the bit about the deaths being random. I'd barely started, though, when my lights flickered and dimmed, and in the darkness I faltered.

You have talked. The words were less than voice but more than wind, and I understood.

You have talked and talked and talked and lied and

lied and lied. It became more like a voice as it went on, and as its resemblance to a human voice increased it sounded increasingly pissed off. The wind on my neck felt like the brush of cold fingers.

You are nothing. You are a liar. Go away.

I took a deep breath. And another. I steadied myself. "Statistically speaking—"

LIAR!

The light bulbs shattered and went out and the wind blew hard enough to make the plane's wreckage groan. I felt cold, dead fingers around my throat. Alone in the dark, I fled.

IT'S A WONDER I DIDN'T break my neck on the way down. I'd like to claim it was my inherent surefootedness, but it probably had something to do with how smooth the path was thanks to a few hundred hikers over the years. I caught my breath maybe fifty yards downhill and forced myself to stop. I tried three times to persuade my lantern to turn on—ordinarily a simple trick—but ultimately had to make do with my headlamp, which was thankfully still strapped to my sweat-slicked brow.

I dropped the Honda keys when I pulled them from my pocket and jumped at the sound they made when they hit the gravel. I scooped them up along with a handful of twigs and rocks and cold dirt, and managed to drop them again while trying to unlock the door.

I put the car in gear, turned with my arm over the passenger seat to look where I was going out the half-fogged rear window—and lurched forward. I wasn't moving fast but it felt like I'd been kicked by a mule as the car hit the concrete stanchion. There was a second crash, and it was only when I smelled wine that I realized the glove box had popped and the merlot had fallen onto my toolkit.

I took a deep breath, and then another, somewhere between a sob and a laugh.

"All right," I said. "Let's try reverse." I pushed the shift two clicks to *actually* put the Honda in reverse, backed out, and crept down the hill. I focused on keeping my breathing and my hands steady instead of thinking about what had happened, just getting home. I passed one car coming the other way on Hedge Road, and then another. I dimly registered the second car making a U-turn behind me. Then the blue lights came on.

Pulling over wasn't too hard, though it put me partway in the ditch. There were footsteps outside the car, and then I was blinded by a flashlight shined into my window. At a rap on the glass, I cranked it down.

"Evenin', Greg," said Chief Dulac. "Know why I pulled you over?"

I fumbled at a response for a second, then shook my head. "Sorry, Chief, I'm not sure."

"Headlight's out." The harsh Maglite beam swept across the hood to the front right where I'd hit the stanchion. "You looked a little unsteady out there. You been drinking tonight, Greg?"

I sighed without meaning to. "No, sir, I just had a problem with my glove box latch."

"Step out of the car, please."

He stepped back and waited with his light on me while I unbuckled and got out. On the bright side, the stop was doing wonders to distract me.

Chief Dulac peered into the car and I could hear him sniffing. The blue-and-whites danced off the Honda's windows and lit up the road. "I talked to Reverend Philips a little while ago. Called off the hunt for her daughter. Said she was up at your place. Anything I ought to know?"

"She came up without a coat. I made her

some coffee and she helped me finish making an apple pie. Sort of. She said if I called her mom she'd leave, and I persuaded her to text her mom instead and let her know she was OK. At least, she said she did."

Chief Dulac kind of grunted. "She texted a friend who we'd been in touch with. We persuaded her friend to ask where she was, and eventually Ashley responded, 'Having pie. Ell. Oh. Ell.' Her friend didn't know what it meant but passed it along. We mentioned it to Mrs. Philips, who said it made sense to her."

"I've been making a lot of pie," I said, and waited for the chief to start the sobriety test or invite me into the back of his cruiser.

"Bring a few slices by the station if you have any spare. Trade you some coffee." This was not an invitation to a bribe, as I'd be coming out ahead in the trade: Chief Dulac's hobby was coffee roasting and he was good at it. He continued, "Get that headlight fixed tomorrow. For now, best get home."

It took me a moment to realize he'd believed me. Unsteady on the road, smelling of wine, with a smashed headlight. That I'd told him the truth didn't make it any less amazing. I had a feeling all of a sudden that Chief Dulac might

have something in common with Adam and
Ashley. Probably useful in his line of work.

"Chief," I said, "you heard I took over from
Joe MacDevitt, right?"

"Yuh?"

"November fifth's coming up."

"Yuh." The change in tone made it clear to
me that he knew exactly what I was talking
about.

"Anyone ever try to do anything about it?"

He snapped off the Maglite and slipped it
into a belt-loop, and then stood a while
illuminated from behind by his cruiser head-
lights and the flickering blues.

"You ever meet my Uncle Frank, Greg?
Father Francis, Catholic priest. Passed away
now, long time ago. When I came on in
Seventy-three, I heard about Nov Five from
Chief Harrison. Persuaded him to call my uncle,
who did an exorcism sort of thing."

"Didn't work?"

He shook his head. "Next Nov Five, three
kids died when their Buick went off the road. It
was ugly." He turned away from me and looked
down at the ground. "Uncle Frank wanted to try
again but Chief said no, and Father Mulligan at
Thomas More agreed. It's just one of those

things, Greg. Nothing for it."

His boots crunched on the gravel as he walked back to the cruiser. "Get that headlight fixed."

I DIDN'T CALL PASTOR JULIE the next day because I didn't know what to say to her, and she didn't call me, presumably for her own reasons. I could guess what they were. I had the vague idea that November first was a religious day, too. Still, I charged up the Infernal Device and took it along, just in case.

I went to get the headlamp taken care of in town; the mechanic looked at it, whistled at the damage, and said it'd be eighty bucks for a new headlight assembly. She'd check the junkyard to see if they had a Honda Civic bumper, but otherwise probably three hundred. It's amazing what two seconds of stupidity can cost. They offered to detail it for me, to clean up the wine, but I figured that was part of my penance. Wiping down my tools had taken most of the morning, and I'd cut myself twice on shards of glass.

Speaking of the cost of stupidity, I barely slept that night. The voice I'd heard at the crash site kept coming back to me, sounding angrier and more human every time. Even awake as I walked into town from the mechanic, I still could hear it in the back of my mind. *Liar!* it kept saying, an accusation instead of a badge of perverse pride.

I ate a late breakfast at the Polkadot, hash browns and eggs. The only pie Dotty had left was apple and I wasn't in the mood. No hot sauce, either. I ate alone and drank a lot of coffee.

I walked back to the garage, but there'd been an emergency and so they hadn't gotten to my car yet and didn't know when they would. I told them I'd bring it back another time.

There'd been two messages on my machine that morning, both jobs. I took care of the Post Office's jammed flagpole pulley and Ms. Lapointe's leaf blower in not much time at all. I went back to the library to see what Gini had turned up for me: obituaries on microfiche going back to the 30s. She taught me how to use the viewing machine and I glanced through them. The November fifth deaths started in 1948, years after the crash. After that, except for Joshua Daniels Carr in 1946, at the age of sixty-three, it was all clear on November fifth in Versailles going back to where the microfiche ran out in 1934.

The article on the crash, written two weeks afterward by a reporter from Berlin, confirmed the date Gini had given. No survivors, crash due to blizzard conditions, etc. Nothing I hadn't heard in Boy Scouts umpteen years ago. I was thanking Gini and returning the microfiche when the Infernal Device rang. I recognized the number as Pastor Julie's church.

I eventually figured out how to answer it, and it was the church secretary.

"Hi, Greg, I tried your house but you weren't there. I hope this is a good time?"

"It's fine, Deb. What's up?"

"Well, I have some sad news. Julia asked me to call you and set up a time to meet. Is Sunday after church all right?"

I thought. That was November third, two days away. "Sure, I'm free. What's wrong?"

"There's been a death, I'm afraid."

"Ashley?" I blurted it out.

"Heavens, no! Goodness, Greg, what gave you that idea? No, Ashley's fine. It's one of her friends from school. They're not releasing the name yet. But the parents will need to select a burial plot, and Julia wasn't sure you knew how that went. Will two o'clock be OK?"

I confirmed the appointment and hung up. "People do die," I told myself. "November first means it's random, just one of those things. Has to happen from time to time."

JAMIE STERLING HAD BEEN T-BONED by a UPS truck while blowing through a stop sign and making a left turn right in front of it. She'd been late for school after sleeping in. If I'd taken the south route into town that morning, I'd have been stuck for half an hour while they cleared it all away.

I drove by that way coming home in the afternoon, pulled over, and got out. There wasn't much danger to me; County Road wasn't heavily traveled outside tourist season. The graying asphalt was strewn with safety glass like coarse sugar. The tire tracks said it all: two parallel lines on the main road where the UPS driver had slammed on the brakes. Four curving lines where Jamie Sterling's car tires had been pushed sideways and then skidded off across the other lane and into the trees, two of which were splintered. More glass, and the smell of gasoline and oil. If she was driving that way to go to school, she must have been one of my neighbors down the hill.

I wasn't sure what I expected to see, or feel. A big bomb symbol? Blood on the pavement, so that I could meditate about whether I had blood on my hands? It was the sort of accident that happened pretty much every day, somewhere. Underneath the word STOP on the sign someone had written "screwing around" in thick black Sharpie. It'd been that way for two years, at least. I stared at it for a while, and looked left at the clear view up the road, then walked back to my car and drove home with the radio off.

Dinner was cold leftovers and warm beer from the cellar. It could have been filet mignon or cardboard for all I noticed. I slept poorly.

The next day was Saturday. Pastor Julie didn't call me, and I didn't call her. I thought about going into town for a newspaper, but didn't. I thought about making myself bacon and eggs for breakfast, but didn't do that, either. I jumped up when there was a knock on the door, but it was just a package delivery, some stuff I'd ordered on Amazon. There was a lot to do around the house and I kept myself busy. I cleaned the gutters, redid the light bulbs since it was sunny, and otherwise sought out whatever manual labor I could. It did not enhance my mental processes, that I could tell. I had a beer, and then a few more, and I fell asleep in my clothes.

I slept late Sunday morning and woke dehydrated and sleep-drunk. The Keurig dribbled and spat black coffee into one cup and then another. I showered, combed my hair, and shaved, and eventually I at least *looked* human. Services would already be over for the morning, and I was halfway down the driveway when I nearly collided with Pastor Julie's truck coming up.

We both slammed on our brakes and skidded to a halt just a few feet from each other. Panting, I looked up to see her pale face staring wide-eyed, and I turned with one arm over the passenger seat and reversed back up the drive.

I stepped out of the car still shaking, and when she jumped down from her cab and looked at me, we both broke into relieved laughter. Before I knew it, she was hugging me tight. I didn't know what propriety demanded under the circumstances, and to hell with propriety anyway. We stood there and I smelled her shampoo and my shoulder got wet and I wondered what was going on but didn't mind too much.

"It's cold out here," she said finally, and

sniffed. I invited her in and ushered her into the kitchen where I set myself to work making a pot of real coffee instead of the machine stuff.

"Have you eaten?" When she said no, I got out a pan and a bowl and a couple eggs. While I cracked them and started whisking, I asked as casually as I could, "What's up?"

"We should talk about the other night."

"I know what it looked like—" I started, but she interrupted me.

"I know nothing happened, Greg. She played me. Us. I realized afterward that she covered herself up when she came back for her bag. She wouldn't have bothered if you'd already… Anyway, after this long I ought to know the difference when she's gotten away with something and when she knows she's busted. She's worse when she tries to pretend she's busted. You still should have called me, though."

"I know."

We silently accepted each other's silent apologies and sat quiet for a while. The coffee pot started gurgling, and I poured us each a cup. "So everything's all right?"

"No. It's not." Julie had never looked that tired before. She sipped her coffee, and I said nothing. "I keep thinking of her as all grown up, and I assume because *I* know I'm willing to listen to her, it automatically makes her comfortable saying anything she needs to. But people don't work that way, and she *is* a person, however often I forget that and try to abstract her away into a problem I need to solve. She's a person who in four years lost her father, got uprooted twice, and is going through all the other teenage garbage at the same time. I'm just sorry you were dragged into it."

"Don't worry about me, I'm all right." I poured the eggs into the pan and swirled them around with a glob of butter. "What about you?"

She shook her head. "I'm hurt, Greg. I don't know what hurts more, that she… did it, or that she thought she *had* to do it just to get her own mother's attention."

"Don't forget that you're a person, too, you know."

She gave a half-laugh. "I try. But I'm a parent and a pastor, and that doesn't leave much time for being a person. I barely get enough sleep as it is."

My chest felt tight, but I said it anyway. "So you and me…"

"Maybe it'd better wait," she said quietly. "I'm not saying no, just maybe we ought to cool down."

"I see," I said. I wanted to argue and say this was important, and maybe I could make her life a little easier, not harder. "Sure, if that's what you want."

I finished the omelet without any more conversation, added some cheddar and a couple apple slices, folded it over and topped it with some more butter. I plated it, said "Hang on," then went into the living room and got the package from Amazon. I tore it open and handed her the big red bottle of Sriracha sauce. Julie laughed.

"I was going to bring it down to the Polka-dot so Dotty could surprise you."

Her smile turned wistful. She drew a lace pattern on the omelet with the sauce, paused for a moment with her eyes closed, and then when she took a bite, a look of bliss crossed her face. "Mmmm. Perfect." I never knew her to talk with her mouth full, and she seemed to realize it, too, because she put her left hand in front of her face while she swallowed. "Thank you."

I tore off a paper towel for use as a napkin—nothing but the finest at Chez Kellogg—and I finished my coffee while she wolfed the omelet.

"I needed that, thank you." She wiped her mouth with the napkin and looked down at the plate. "We also need to talk about the arrangements for Jamie Sterling's funeral." She took a deep breath. "And Father Michaels might be in touch about Drew Leclerc now, too."

"Who?"

"Our neighbor down the street. His oldest boy had their car up on blocks to change a tire or something this morning, and it rolled on him. Ashley's there now, watching the two youngest." She drank some coffee and the cup trembled in her hand.

"I'm sorry," I said.

She acknowledged it with a distracted nod. "I talked a little bit about Jamie in church today. I wasn't feeling very original, I'm afraid. I'm not that good at it. I never know what to say about the dead."

"I'm sure you're fine," I said.

"Funny thing for a preacher, to be tongue-tied about death. I didn't know what to say to Ashley when Tom's cancer got bad, or when he passed away. I thought Divinity School would teach me everything I needed to know, but… Jamie and Drew, back to back like that."

I started to mumble a protest but she talked over me. "I was there when they found him, Greg. I helped pull the car off his body. I can still see it when I shut my eyes. T-shirt and jeans even though it's not even forty degrees out there. He was holding a wrench, and he'd drawn one of those stupid bombs on his wrist in ballpoint pen. He had this look of complete surprise, like he couldn't believe what had just happened to him. His parents were right there, trying to keep his brothers inside the house. I didn't know what to say."

I sat back, stunned.

"We lie to ourselves," she said. "I lie to them. Every town like Versailles thinks it's Lake Wobegon, that everyone's strong, wise, and above average, and that it's *all going to be OK.* We tell ourselves that we're good people doing our best—*I* tell them we're good people doing our best—but are we?"

I thought about fleeing in the dark from an angry voice, about being terrified enough to ram a concrete pole. "I think," I said carefully, "we tell ourselves all that in the hopes that if we do it often enough, it'll be true when we need it to be."

She played in the remains of the Sriracha

with her fork, not looking at me. "So I'm not lying to them, I'm just telling the truth prematurely?"

"Something like that."

"Something like that," she repeated back to me, her expression pensive. Then she nodded to herself and sat up straighter in her chair, and we got down to the business of planning a burial.

JOE CALLED ME TO COME in on the third knock. His living room had been pushed around a bit to make the walking areas wider, and the fishing tackle had been cleaned up. Joe himself hobbled into the room on a Zimmer-frame walker with split tennis balls on the front legs.

"Hey, Greg, quitting already? Grab a seat. You want coffee?"

I laughed, said no to the quitting and yes to the coffee, and Joe disappeared again back into the kitchen. I suppressed the urge to go help: no sense irritating him too soon. I valiantly ignored the crash, since it wasn't loud enough to be Joe and didn't sound like glass. "Can I help carry something?" I called back when it sounded like the coffee pot was sputtering.

In the end I wound up joining him at the kitchen table with a mug of hot black coffee that tasted like jet fuel. Joe put out a big sugar bowl with a soup spoon in it but didn't take any himself.

"So listen, Joe. It's November third today."

"Yuh." He eyed me. "So it is."

"Almost November fifth."

He stared into the steaming coffee.

"What I don't get, Joe, is why isn't the whole town aware of this? For Pete's sake, the high school teachers must have noticed something."

He shrugged. "Who remembers dates? The police took twenty years to notice. Probably the older teachers know, sure, but they wouldn't talk about it. Some things get around a small town. Some things don't." Joe shook his head. "I apologize, Greg. I shouldn't have mentioned it to you. Getting it gradually means you wouldn't be having damn fool ideas that you could do something about it."

"Maybe I am, maybe I'm not. I just want to ask a few questions."

Joe shifted in his ladder-back chair and glanced at his Zimmer frame. He wasn't in much shape for running away, and anyway, where would he retreat to?

"I've seen the bomb stencils, Joe. Nobody's doing that, are they?"

He shook his head.

"They just appear, right?"

He nodded, and drank his coffee. I took a deep breath.

"I screwed up, Joe. I need to know how bad."

When he kept staring into his coffee, I continued. "I went up to the plane to talk to it." He looked up at me then, with a flash of—confusion, maybe? "I thought I could do something about it. Maybe reason with it."

Joe shut his eyes and rubbed his forehead. "You pissed it off."

"And now someone's dead."

"Someone was already gonna die, Greg, that's what I was trying to tell you."

"It's November *third*, Joe. And I think it killed someone on the first, too. I think I *really* pissed it off."

"Shit." He shook his head and made a vague gesture with his left hand. He opened his mouth like he was going to say something, then shut it again. "Shit."

"Tell me what happened, Joe."

He looked into his coffee. "Plane crash. You said it yourself."

I felt bad about pushing the old guy. I liked

him a lot, but I needed information.

"Something's been bugging me, Joe. How did they know the altimeter broke? Gini at the library knows the official story down pat, and the official story is that the altimeter broke. But I've seen the wreck, there's no way they'd have been able to tell after the crash. And it wasn't in the paper. Plus, it's the wrong day."

"Don't know about that."

"Tell me about the spy, then."

He blanched and had to put his coffee cup down. "I was only eleven, Greg. I didn't have anything to do with it."

"But you know."

"Yeah, I know." He waved vaguely at the cabinet past the fridge. "I need something a little stronger than this. Would you?"

I got down the half-empty bottle of Chivas Regal and handed it over. He put a healthy shot in his coffee and passed it back. I don't care for Scotch, but in the interest of being comradely I added a nip to my own.

He took a sip and grimaced. "His name was Bull Kelly. *Captain* Kelly. One of those big, blond, cornfed types from out Nebraska. We all heard the plane. Damnation, those are loud. In my recollections, it made a huge noise when it crashed, but I don't know if it really did. I remember the fire, though, and everyone going out in the blizzard to see the mountain burning. The fire truck came out, but I don't think they had any idea what to do about it. We were there quite a while. There was a war on, remember, and we were even more isolated then than we are now. We didn't know if it was one of ours or theirs or if we were under attack or what."

I wondered why on earth anyone thought Germany might attack Versailles, New Hampshire, but I kept quiet.

"And then," Joe said, "out of the woods stumbles Bull Kelly, dazed and exhausted, but not a scratch on him. Luckiest sonofabitch in the world, and boy did he know it. For a little kid like me, he was Superman. Someone put him up for the night and they tried to get through to the Army, but the telephone lines were out and it wasn't safe to drive."

He took another long drink of doctored coffee, and then another. I had a sip of mine, and it wasn't bad, but I didn't want to get tipsy.

"Bull was real popular with us kids right away, we were real taken with him. He'd been a bombardier in Europe and he told us all these stories about flying missions over Germany. The older girls liked him, too, and even I could tell that he liked those girls right back.

"Some of the older boys didn't appreciate that last part too much, and they decided to teach him a lesson. They jumped him, wanted to kind of beat him up. I'm not sure exactly how he died, but I have a feeling he was more hurt in the crash than he let on. It was an accident, anyway."

"I never heard any of this," I said.

Joe shook his head. "Neither did the Army. Took another few days for the roads to clear, and by then the town had decided to hush it up and let everyone think he died in the crash or in the woods. Must have been hard work digging that grave, but they did it. Told us kids to keep quiet—loose lips sink ships and all that—and anyway, the Army guys never talked to us when they came out to have a look. We kinda got the idea that meant he was a spy. The older boys who'd jumped him all enlisted right away, and none of them came home."

We sat in silence for a while, drinking our doctored coffees and thinking our own thoughts. I was getting an inkling of why I'd pissed it off so much. I just wasn't sure what to do about it.

NATHANIEL "BULL" KELLY'S GRAVE IS at the back of the Stonewall Cemetery grounds, where there isn't actually a wall, just some big rocks where the hills become too stony and crooked even for burying the dead. It's an unmarked granite slab, erected some time in the 50s the first time one of Joe's and my predecessors put two and two together about the dates. No graffiti, despite generations of teenagers hanging out, and no bomb markings. Plenty of cigarette butts, though, and some beer bottles, which I set to collecting while I considered my next move.

The sense of hostility was hard to miss as I approached. I didn't say anything, though, and the feeling of anger didn't get worse. I'd brought a white plastic garbage bag and shoveled in the bottles and butts and a half-finished homework paper covered in algebra. The bottles clanked in the bottom while I wandered around busying myself.

It was cold out, I wanted to be elsewhere, and I was jittery—though, that could have been all the coffee I'd drunk that morning. I needed to think, and this felt like the best place to get some focus. I tied off the red plastic straps on the bag, set it down on the ground, and stood with my arms crossed as I looked at the unmarked granite.

It was tempting to give up. I had no plan and my last attempt had gone bad. Wiser men than me had tried and failed. I knew a little more than I did before, and a liar ought to be able to make use of that, to find the loose part of the knot and tug for all he's worth, but I couldn't see it. The lie implied a liar: three-quarters of a century of buried guilt and coincidences seemed a powerful enough liar to me. A murdering ghost was a nasty lie, but it *was* a lie. If there was a thread in there, though, I didn't have it.

Anyone passing by must have wondered at me, pacing back and forth in front of the grave, stamping hard to warm myself up. Bull Kelly wasn't much company, but he didn't appear to object to me marching around while I plotted his downfall. I figured if I tortured myself long enough, I might get two brain cells to rub together and come up with something good. Eventually they did. It wasn't a way to wipe the whole thing out, but it might just be a way to beat it. Maybe only once, but once was enough. I could live with once.

The trouble was, the plan required Julie's

help and Ashley's cooperation, and neither one would be easy to get. I tromped up the hill in the cold, taking the shortcut through the briars. I went to the phone without taking my boots off, and called their home. Julie answered.

"It's Greg," I said. "We need to talk about November fifth."

It took a little finagling, but she drove up to the house to see me. While I got ready for her to come over, I rehearsed what I was going to say, but in the end it spilled out in a gush: how far back the deaths went, the bomber crash and Bull Kelly, and how he died, and the neighborhood kids calling him a spy. I'd done some research on the Internet, too, and found the death dates of the local boys who hadn't come back from the war: I wasn't surprised. Her expression was pained, and I could tell she thought I'd gone off the deep end. I took a long breath and went deeper.

"I think it's my fault that Jamie Sterling and Drew Leclerc died."

She frowned. "Greg, that's not possible."

"I pissed it off. I went up to the wreckage before I knew enough, and I tried to undo it."

"Undo? Greg. Stop this, you're not making sense."

"I'm a liar, Julie."

She winced. "Now wait a—"

"Not like that. Hang on." I'd thought this through beforehand and was prepared. I opened the top drawer on the island and pulled out the lit light bulb. Julie looked puzzled as I handed it to her, and it obviously hurt her to look right at it.

"I did that. It's a regular light bulb, and I persuaded it to make light on its own."

"Come on, Greg. It's cute, but you can buy those off Amazon. They have LEDs in them."

I took it back, put it on the counter, and hit it with my shoe. She gasped as it shattered, then stared at the hundred shining pieces.

"They'll go out in a minute," I said. "And there's this."

On the stove was a simmering pot of water. I fished out the gravel at the bottom with a skimmer and dumped it into a metal bowl. The wet gravel clinked and scraped as I took three scoopfuls. The bowl frosted in the steamy air. I put it down and plucked out a piece which was as cold as though I'd taken it from the freezer. I held it out to Julie, who only looked at it.

"I don't get it."

"I told those rocks they were cold. They

were in my driveway at the time and it's cold out, so it wasn't too hard to do. Took five minutes to convince them, and it'll last another hour. Useful when I go into town for ice cream." She finally picked one up between two fingers, then dropped it.

"Show me how you do it," she said.

I looked around the kitchen for a minute, then took down a long wooden spoon from the jumble of utensils in the coffee can next to the stove. I passed it to her to examine, and she shrugged at it. I broke it over my knee, fitted the halves back together, and spoke to it under my breath. Nothing fancy, and I didn't bother to smooth down the splinters, so when I was done it had kind of a wood fringe like a lion's mane, but was whole again.

I passed it over and she spent a minute trying to torque it—tentatively at first, then putting her weight into it.

I said, "You believe in life after death."

She blinked, but was on firmer ground there. She put down the spoon. "Yes, I do."

"So the notion of a ghost, an angry ghost? An angry ghost killing people from beyond the grave?"

"Is childish."

"It's a lie. An awful lie."

She pursed her lips. "You could put it that way."

"The light bulb, the coldstones, the spoon—those are lies, too. I persuaded the world to be the way I wanted it to be. This ghost is like that. I can undo lies like these, and I thought I could do the same with Bull Kelly. I went up on Halloween night after you left. I was frustrated and wanted to do something to help, and I screwed up. Jamie and Drew paid the price."

She didn't look at me, but stared instead down at the glass fragments. They were going out, but not as fast as I'd expected.

"I want you to have Ashley stay home from school tomorrow. Keep her home, keep her safe."

"Why?"

I didn't answer her right away. Instead, I took Adam's doodles from another drawer. She narrowed her eyes at them. "My brother drew these in the days before he died. He just up and started one day. November fifth, 1981, he walked out on ice he knew for sure was safe to walk on and went right through. Just like Jamie Sterling was sure it was safe to make that left, and Drew Leclerc thought it was safe to get under the car. You said Drew had drawn that bomb symbol on his hand."

"You saw Ashley's tattoo."

I nodded.

"You think that means she's a target."

I nodded again. "I think it kills by taking advantage of a sense of safety. My brother Adam had a knack for knowing things, kind of the opposite of what I do. I can fool rocks into staying cold in the oven, but I couldn't ever pull the wool over his eyes. Nobody could. It made him confident."

"Ashley's like that," Julie said. "I always thought she was unusually perceptive, but it was uncanny the way she saw through us when Tom was sick. She knew before I did, I think."

"It makes her an easier target for him, like Adam was. When Adam walked out on that ice, he *knew* he was safe, knew it down in his bones."

"Just like Bull Kelly knew he was in the clear the minute he walked off that mountain," she said.

I stopped, surprised. "Yeah," I said. "I hadn't thought of it that way."

"So I should keep her home? And she'll be safe?"

"More than that, I hope. I think it made a

mistake targeting her instead of picking someone off at random. Someone with her talents is an easier target, but if she survives, it will have been proved wrong. It might stop killing altogether, or it might give me the opening I need to take care of it. But even if none of those things is true, I think keeping her safe for the day will make her safe from Bull Kelly for good."

JULIE LEFT ON THE FOURTH without committing herself to my scheme. But she called me on the afternoon of the fifth and said she could use some company; she didn't have to ask twice. I parked behind her truck in the driveway.

She welcomed me in with a mug of coffee. "Fresh brewed," she said. "Ashley's upstairs." As if on cue, loud jangly music came on. "She thinks I'm weird, but she won't look a gift sick day in the mouth. Besides, after losing two classmates, I think she could use some time to herself."

I took off my jacket, then laid it over the back of the couch. Julie got out a deck of cards and we went into the kitchen to sit at her big pine table with our coffee mugs, where we'd see if Ashley got it into her head to climb out her window. "I was watching TV," she explained, "but it's hard to concentrate. Do you play gin rummy?"

I did, if not well. She dealt us ten cards each and we set to playing.

Under the circumstances, I think I should be excused for paying more attention to her than to my cards. She hadn't slept, I was pretty sure: her hair was swept back in a frizzled ponytail and there were dark circles under her eyes.

I don't think either of us won any hands so much as held off losing longer. We didn't keep score, but I expect she was ahead by a hand or two. Every thump overhead made us both jump.

We looked out at their backyard, which was getting dark. I always hated that about fall evenings, how early the sun set. I can deal with dark, and I can deal with cold, but cold *and* dark get to me after a while. We watched the shadows stretch and merge into the dark.

"I feel like I'm standing guard," she said.

"I think she understands. She's a bright kid."

"I don't know if *I* understand, Greg. But what's a day off school in the grand scheme of things, really?"

"Well, if I'd skipped one day less, I'd be a doctor now."

She narrowed her eyes. "You're not help-ing." I just smiled. "Do you think we'll know if this works? I mean, aside from me having a living, breathing daughter tomorrow morning."

I considered that. "Well, I could go back up to the crash or out to the grave and try some fancy lies. See if something objects along the lines of the other night."

"Isn't that dangerous?"

"For me? I don't think so. Or do you mean, is it possible to revive this thing?" I sipped my coffee. "I don't know, to be honest. But I think I might be able to tell if it's gone." I explained the Wile E. Coyote feeling and she snorted, but said she got the idea.

She finished her coffee and slapped the table with both palms. "You know what I want? Ice cream."

"Sounds good."

"It does! And darn it, what's the point of being an adult if you can't have ice cream when you want it?"

"No point at all, seems to me."

"Glad you agree," she said with a manic grin. "Why don't you run to Doug's and get some?"

I'd been hornswoggled.

I got my jacket and went to put it on, then stopped myself. It took me a second to realize I hadn't heard the jingle of keys in the pocket. I went through all the pockets, earning a puzzled look from Julie. No keys.

I went to the window and peered to the end of their long driveway. No Honda, either.

"'THIS IS STUPID,'" JULIE READ the Post-It note aloud. "'I'm fine. Be back late, don't do anything I wouldn't do. Luv, Ash'" We were standing in Ashley's room, with her music still playing. We felt dumb that she'd gotten past us without us hearing, but glad she hadn't gone out the window; a broken neck would have suited Bull Kelly's purposes just fine.

Julie called Ashley's cell phone; no answer. She called the parents whose phone numbers she knew. I overheard the word "again" a lot. After calling the last parent, she drummed her fingers on the table and called the police to ask them to keep an eye out. She left her cell number, then we pulled on our jackets and got into her truck.

The sidewalks roll up early in Versailles and there wasn't really anywhere to go, but we drove into town anyway and looked for my car or its driver. One of the problems with driving a silver Honda Civic is that pretty much every car on the road looks like it, and we got tired of false alarms pretty quick.

"If we can't find her," I said at a stop sign after taking three streets to work myself up to it, "I want to try again to undo it."

She didn't give any indication that she'd heard me. But after we'd been on the road for half an hour, we slowed down at the cemetery. The gate was shut, and I could see from the car that it was locked, but that hadn't stopped kids in the past. Julie parked the truck and turned the key.

At that point, we'd tried everywhere in town. She might have gone to Berlin, or some of her friends' parents had cabins up by Lake Umbagog, but neither of us thought it likely.

"I don't like this," Julie said.

"Me neither."

I opened the gate's ice-cold Yale lock with shaking hands, and behind me Julie said, "Shit."

I turned and looked at her.

"My phone's dead. I thought I plugged it into the charger. Maybe I should go back to the house."

I rummaged my pockets for the Infernal

Device. To my credit, I had remembered to bring it. I had not remembered to charge it.

"All right," I said, "come back for me in an hour."

Julie walked up to join me instead. "There's no point," she explained. "Either something has happened or it hasn't. People know to look for her. Charging my phone won't make a difference."

We took the path slowly.

"What are you going to do?" she asked.

"Mostly what I planned to do last time. I know more now, and that'll make a difference."

We walked. Tendrils of fog curled around the gravestones and our feet. Usually I liked the fog and would recite that Carl Sandburg poem to myself. But that night the fog crept in on lizard claws and when it sat on its haunches I bet it was licking its lips. I found myself dreading what I'd set myself to do. It'd been one thing back when it was a vague lie built from superstition. Putting a name to it made me uneasy.

Julie cleared her throat. "You said Henry told you that a lie implies a liar. In those words?"

"Yuh."

"But you also said he preferred the word

'persuasion' for what you do."

"Sure."

"So, was he *telling* you that a lie implies a liar? Or arguing against your terminology?"

"Well, he—" I blinked. "I mean, he— I don't know."

"Because, it seems odd that he would object to your calling it 'lying' and then use the term himself. Wouldn't he have said a persuasion implies a persuader?"

She had a point there, but it wasn't making me any happier about my chances of success.

Hello… Liar…

I stopped short when I heard that and found myself standing a few feet from the Spy's Tomb—from Bull Kelly's grave. Julie came up beside me.

Stop annoying me, the voice said. It was stronger than before, had personality to it. I was kinda hard-pressed to consider that a good sign. *There's nothing you can do.*

"Greg?" She gave me a worried look. "What's going on?"

"Can't you hear that?"

"I… I don't know if this will work."

"It's all right," I said, not one hundred percent sure that was true. "I can do this."

I had an idea, however half-baked, of how to go about it this time. Knowing the name, knowing what the people in town had done, knowing from the Internet what the actual odds were of flipping heads seventy times in a row. And, critically, hoping Ashley was still alive, both for her own sake and because if she was alive that long into November fifth, then I had the piece I was lacking before. If she were dead, I was about to get myself into very deep trouble.

"I did some reading on statistics," I said aloud, casually. I wasn't lying yet, I was laying groundwork.

Run away again, liar. I liked that. Julie's eyes got wide, and I figured she heard it that time, too.

"The odds against flipping a coin heads seventy times in a row are astronomical," I continued. "One in ten to the twenty-one, can you believe that? Big number. Can't get my head around it, personally. But the funny thing is, those are the same odds of flipping a coin heads sixty-nine times in a row, and then one tails. The exact same."

I took a breath and pulled my jacket tighter around me, though it didn't do much against the cold wind. I hadn't said anything untrue yet, but it was reacting like I had. The murmur on the air got louder and the wind grew colder.

"It's pretty weird, I guess, all these November fifth deaths. Odds against that look pretty high."

I glanced at Julie. Her face was tight, and I hated to say more. I knew what she must be thinking, about Ashley, and I was afraid if I went on and something had happened to her that she might never forgive me. But I did, trying my damnedest to keep my voice conversational.

"But you gotta die of something. People die all the time, here and everywhere else. It's like flipping a coin every day. Heck of a coin, but still. There's probably a town out there where someone dies every year on Christmas—wouldn't that be a kick in the teeth? New York City or Tokyo, someone probably dies once an hour. It doesn't mean there's some kind of *ghost*, it's just probability. Just math. And once you wake yourself up and realize you don't *need* a ghost—well!"

The wind came up suddenly and pushed me strong on the chest until I stumbled back. I grinned and made an exaggerated, "Brr!" noise. The grin wasn't too honest, though. It wasn't forming words anymore, but the cold wind didn't let up. The important thing was to not acknowledge him. If I could keep going in that vein, whatever it was that thought of itself as Bull Kelly would fade away. Probably.

"It's, uh, funny how people anthropomorphize the strangest things. Just human nature, I guess. I read on the Internet someone saw Elvis on a piece of toast. Sold it for a hundred bucks on the eBay, isn't that something? That's, um…" I cleared my throat and realized I'd raised my voice. Above my head, pine boughs creaked. "Boy, that's something. But just because we anthropomorphize toast, doesn't make it human. It, uh, it doesn't stand up. Take—"

"Greg, stop."

I stopped myself, almost falling; I hadn't realized I'd drawn myself up on tiptoes. The angry muttering got louder as my concentration broke. A guy more interested in excuses might have been glad for that one right then.

Julie looked miserable.

"I know it's risky," I said, "but—"

"It's not working, Greg. I don't know anything about what you do, but everything I do know is telling me this can't work. A ghost may be a lie, but it's a lie who thinks he's a person.

You can't just make people go away, Greg."

"I don't know if I can do this any other way," I said. Something swept against my cheek and I forced myself to picture a leaf.

She stared down at the ground, not at me. I had to strain to hear what she said next. "Then maybe we shouldn't."

I knew what it took her to say that, and we both knew what it meant. We stood quiet for a while in the biting wind with groans and pops sounding from the trees.

"All right," I said. "Let's try reverse."

It took me a moment to get my bearings. I wasn't used to having to do something so complicated on the spur of the moment, and I'd have given a lot just then for five minutes to sit and think. But damn it all, I was the liar who drove a bone-dry Honda three miles and whose house was lit by mendacious sunshine. I could do this.

"You know, Bull Kelly, I believe we got off on the wrong foot. And I apologize for that, I do. My name's Greg Kellogg, and I'm a bit of a fibber."

I planted my feet and stuck my hands in my pockets and just smiled into the wind. It bit like blackflies and I couldn't feel my ears anymore, which was probably for the best.

"I found a picture of you, by the way. You looked sharp in that uniform. Handsome." I described the uniform as best I could, drawing on the photos I'd seen in the library and on museum exhibits. As I talked about it, we saw it take shape in the fog. Just a bit of brown here and there, then the brass buttons. By the time I got to the silver bombardier's wings I could see it like rocks at the bottom of a pond.

"Yuh," I said. "Damn sharp. You're a brave fella, volunteering to fly those rickety old things to fight the Nazis. Bombardier's a hard job. Dangerous. I looked it up, you know. I'm afraid of heights myself, I couldn't sit there with nothing between me and the ground but a little Plexiglas and some straps."

The uniform stood straighter as I talked. I described the man himself as he'd been in those old photos. Blond, Joe had said. Big, blond, cornfed type, taking shape as I talked. I stopped describing him when he folded his arms in front of his chest, the first overt movement the figure made.

"Damnation, you're tall." I stepped forward into the fog, so close I could see the ribbons on his chest, which weren't much lower than eye level to me. Behind the ribbons I could see the grave, dimly. Somewhere in the back of my mind, I was very impressed with myself.

"Look at yourself, Bull. I mean it, just look at yourself." I cajoled him until he finally, slowly, brought up his translucent hands, and as he stared, the color came into them. "I coulda used a fella like you when I was fixing my roof last summer. Up and down that ladder in the hot sun with a bucket of nails or a bundle of flashing. Scraped up my hands a bit. Got sunburned, too."

I went on in that vein, talking about all the chores I'd have put him to around the house. I've a pretty good running list, so that part wasn't hard. The trick was skipping the ones that weren't physical—no paying the electric bill, no phone calls. Painting and weeding, lifting and carrying and squatting down. I talked about backaches and sore muscles and sunburns and poison ivy and sore joints: topics any good Yankee can go on about for hours. Bull Kelly went from translucent like smoke to translucent like glass, and more to the point I had him thinking solid as he started to kinda nod along.

"And that's just the house. This place could use some upkeep, too. If you could scrub out the coffeepot, that'd be a kindness. Not a lot of work, you just got to get your elbow into it." I mimicked the action, moving my whole arm.

The look on his face was stony before, but had now gone from grave-like stillness to boredom. Useful thing, boredom. You get somebody interested in something, they forget all about themselves. You bore someone silly, though, and they notice every itch and ache and gurgle. Julie yawned a little and then Bull did, too, and I knew I'd arrived.

"Yuh," I said. "You look like a solid, capable guy. There's just one thing you're not capable of, really. Causing accidents anymore."

His expression went from bored to puzzled. I pointed way up above me to the big pine bough.

"Don't believe me? Make that branch come down. Bring it down on my head." I bent over and pointed to where my hair was thinning. "No protection, see?"

I looked him square in the face, quashing any hint of fear that I might not be anything but a hundred percent right. He opened his mouth and I heard something on the wind—I hadn't thought to talk about talking, but too late for that now—and a look of fury crossed his face. I had him.

"I'd say you lost the knack, but I'm thinking you never really had it. It was all statistics in the first place. Either way, no more killing, Bull Kelly. You can't do all that, any more than—" I caught myself before making the comparison to myself. "Any more than Pastor Julie here could. Have you met Julie, Bull? Smart lady, smarter than either one of us, probably both put together. She made me realize that you don't win a fight like this by making your opponent less human, you win by making him more so. A vague idea of an angry ghost might be able to thin ice and wreck cars, but—"

I haven't taken a punch since fourth grade, and Jenny Paquin didn't have Bull Kelly's right hook. I hit the ground hard and my head was swimming so much I thought I was going to throw up. I scrambled back on my hands, scratching my palms as I pushed with my boot heels. But he only stood there instead of coming after me, heaving air he wasn't breathing, flexing his fingers like he wanted to wring my neck.

Julie helped me stand and we stood there together as Nathaniel Kelly sat heavily on his grave, stunned. He stared down at his translucent hands sticking out of uniform sleeves. Back in the habit of thinking of himself as a person, he couldn't shake it.

"I guess I had that coming," I said. "For what it's worth, you deserved better than you got. I'm sorry. I am. But it's time for you to move on."

I ought to have felt elated, I suppose. I'd never pulled off a lie like that, and with any luck I never would again. Mostly I was exhausted, and my face hurt. Julie hung back when I turned to leave.

"We're not done," she said. "We can't leave him like this." She returned to the log she'd been sitting on and settled herself down again with her hands folded on her knees. "Nathaniel."

He looked up and spoke, but his voice was just a whisper on the wind. She strained to hear and repeated his name. She looked up at me and asked if there was anything I could do.

I frowned, and thought. Lies work better with expected forms, the reason I used light bulbs for light instead of duct tape. I did have one idea, and I wasn't sure if I was amused or horrified. I took the Infernal Device from my pocket and whispered a few words to it.

Bull Kelly responded angrily to the lie in his

presence, but the wind didn't pick up or anything; he just glared. I listened until I was sure I was hearing his swearing from the phone speaker. It lit up despite the dead battery, which I considered a touch on the spooky side.

Julie reached out a shaking hand and took it from me. With an expression on her face somewhere between dread and disgust, she held it to her ear, absent-mindedly pulling back a few strands of hair. "Nathaniel?"

She looked ill just then, with her face lit up by the screen. Her apprehension turned into a wan little smile as she glanced up at me. "I'm Julie Philips. How do you do?"

I STOOD GUARD AT A respectful distance for a while—I don't rightly remember how long, but by the time I decided she wasn't in any danger I could help with and started to wander around, the air had gotten bitterly cold and still. Nothing supernatural, just November. I started to stomp my feet to warm myself, but it made my head hurt and I worried about making noise, so I wound up pacing back and forth between the headstones.

I worried about Julie but could still hear her calm voice. She even laughed once. After a while worrying, I started to feel dumb just pacing. I wondered whether I should run and fetch her the Mylar emergency blanket from the truck and then whether I had finished off the pie in the fridge. I thought about going to the cottage to make coffee, but didn't want to wander too far. Mostly I couldn't keep my mind off the light bulbs and the glove box latch. And all my other lies that wore off.

It felt like forever but was probably about an hour. I heard Julie before I saw her, tromping through soggy leaves and rubbing her arms with her hands to warm up.

"It's over," she said, and handed me the Infernal Device. She'd turned it off, which I expect was for the best. "He's gone. He called you a liar and an idiot and said to say thank you."

We took the path slowly; she was so tired she could barely walk straight, and I might have been a little on the sleepy side myself.

We had to concentrate on the path to get to the gate without falling and breaking our necks, but about a million years later the iron gate materialized out of the fog in front of us.

"What did he say?" I asked as I let us out.

She shook her head. "What a guy says to his

pastor ought to be private, alive or dead."

I locked the gate while she unlocked the passenger door for me.

"He really called me an idiot?"

She shrugged and I thought I saw a faint smile cross her lips as she turned the ignition. "We talked about a lot of things."

"Did he call *you* an idiot?"

She pursed her lips, but her eyes were definitely smiling. "What a guy says to his pastor ought to be private."

We pulled onto the main road, driving slowly because the fog was starting to get thick.

"You haven't talked about Ashley," I said as gently as I could. She gripped the steering wheel a little tighter.

"She wasn't his target. Had no idea who she was."

It wasn't until a lot later that I realized how much danger I'd put *myself* in with my assumption, and later still that I realized she'd gotten the idea of the tattoo from me back when I called her attention to it in the graveyard. At the time, I just exhaled. "So she's safe."

She laughed, once, without humor. "She's driving around at night in a stolen car on foggy back roads full of deer, probably with her stupid friends along for the ride and determined to prove that she's not in any danger. Who needs Bull Kelly?"

I looked at the trees go by outside the window. A speed limit sign passed, white in the fog. "Whatever happens, you did a good thing back there."

She kept her eyes on the road, but fumbled for my hand and gave it a squeeze.

Her house lights were all still off and there was a police car idling out front, dark except for the computer screen inside. Julie slowed down and drove with her hands clenching the wheel. We didn't say anything, just parked and got out of the car and walked over to where Chief Dulac was getting out of his cruiser. Julie took my hand and squeezed it again.

"Evening, Reverend. Evening, Greg."

Julie's voice came out as a rasp. "Ashley?"

"She's fine, ma'am." The pressure on my hand relaxed. "She's in a holding cell. Saw her driving with a busted headlight. Car smelled of alcohol. She said she had your permission to drive it, but I couldn't get through on your phone, so I brought her in. I took the opportunity to have a little heart-to-heart talk with the young lady."

"Thank you," Julie managed.

"Car's at the impound lot, Greg. I'll ask in the morning if you're pressing charges."

I was about to say right then that I wouldn't, but Julie squeezed my hand a third time.

Chief Dulac glanced up at the house. "Been a quiet night so far."

"I think," I said, "there's a good chance it'll stay that way."

He looked me in the eye, looked at Julie, then back to me. After a while he started nodding. "Good." He tore a ticket off his pad and handed it to me. "I told you to get that light fixed."

"Yessir."

"Have a good night, folks."

He drove away, and after the shock of relief wore off we got back into the truck so Julie could drive me home. It was a short trip, and we listened to the jazz show on the radio in companionable silence.

Julie walked me to my door, and we stopped. She looked at me for a long time, and I looked at her, and I noticed we were standing somewhat on the close side. She leaned in even closer, looked into my eyes, and then shook my hand and said, "Good night, Mr. Kellogg."

…Have I mentioned that I'm a liar?

Acknowledgements

A lot of people helped this little book out into the world. First and foremost, the team at The Liar's first home, The Magazine of Science Fiction and Fantasy. Without CC Finlay, Gordon van Gelder and Lisa Rogers, you may not have ever gotten to read this story, and it certainly wouldn't have been as good. An enormous thank you to them.

This novella started life in the Codex Writers Group, with wonderful feedback from the participants of the 2014 novella contest. I particularly wanted to thank Vylar Kaftan and Caroline M. Yoachim for their support and feedback as I got ready to send poor Greg out into the wide world. Thank you, too, to Jeffe Kennedy, Jon Brazee, and Erin Hartshorn for their extensive advice in getting this standalone edition published and into your hands.

I would also like to thank the many people who have supported this little story as it made its way: my friends and family who cheered it on, readers and reviewers who took the time to tell me how much they enjoyed it, and the Nebula voters who so kindly remembered my story when award season came.

Finally, thank you to Liz, who put up with a frankly ridiculous amount of fretting and thinking-out-loud and an epic level of procrastination that culminated in the production of an eight foot long green felt squid (using her office and her sewing equipment).

About the Author

John P. Murphy is an engineer and writer who's been living in New Hampshire for going on two decades now. His short fiction has appeared in venues including The Magazine of Fantasy and Science Fiction, Nature Futures, Daily Science Fiction, and the Drabblecast.

Links to his online fiction and public appearances can be found at JohnPMurphy.net.

Made in the USA
Monee, IL
17 July 2020